"I need to talk to you, Ryder."

She looked around the room nervously and then turned her gaze back to him. "Can we go somewhere quieter? Somewhere we can be alone?"

He nodded, his mind playing cruel tricks on him, making him remember things better forgotten. He hadn't seen or heard from Kathi in almost two years. Not a phone call. Not a card. Nothing but the secret baby girl she'd had someone else deliver to his doorstep.

Now she was back, just as unexpectedly as she'd left. That could only mean one thing. "Is this about the baby?"

"Promise me you can keep my baby safe."

"Betsy is my daughter, too, Kathi." Ryder's voice was intense, his eyes dark and embracing. "I'd go to the grave to protect her." He traced a finger down her cheek, and the searing heat of his touch attacked the frigid walls around her heart. "And, just so you'll know, I'd go to the grave to protect you as well."

Dear Harlequin Intrigue Reader,

Harlequin Intrigue serves up its romance with a generous dash of suspense, so sit back and feast on this month's selections!

Joanna Wayne continues her RANDOLPH FAMILY TIES miniseries with an exciting flourish in *A Mother's Secrets* (#577). Gayle Wilson brings another of her sexy, mysterious heroes to life in *Renegade Heart* (#578), the second title in her MORE MEN OF MYSTERY series. Look for the final installment in November.

We're delighted to introduce debut author Ann Voss Peterson and her book, *Inadmissible Passion* (#579). After someone tried to kill her, Brittany Gerritsen turned to the one man she vowed to stay away from—the man who called off their engagement. And our SECRET IDENTITY program heats up with *Little Boy Lost* (#580) by Adrianne Lee. When a look-alike impostor stole Carleen Ellison's identity and her sweet little boy, she had no choice but to turn to Kane Kincaid—her baby's secret father.

As always, Harlequin Intrigue is committed to giving readers the best in romantic suspense and that is a promise you can count on!

Sincerely,

Denise O'Sullivan
Associate Senior Editor
Harlequin Intrigue

A MOTHER'S SECRETS

JOANNA WAYNE

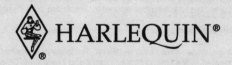

HARLEQUIN®

TORONTO • NEW YORK • LONDON
AMSTERDAM • PARIS • SYDNEY • HAMBURG
STOCKHOLM • ATHENS • TOKYO • MILAN • MADRID
PRAGUE • WARSAW • BUDAPEST • AUCKLAND

ISBN 0-373-22577-6

A MOTHER'S SECRETS

Visit us at www.eHarlequin.com

Printed in U.S.A.

ABOUT THE AUTHOR

Joanna Wayne lives with her husband just a few miles from steamy, exciting New Orleans, but her home is the perfect writer's hideaway. A lazy bayou, complete with graceful herons, colorful wood ducks and an occasional alligator, winds just below her back garden. When not creating tales of spine-tingling suspense and heartwarming romance, she enjoys reading, golfing or playing with her grandchildren and, of course, researching and plotting out her next novel. Taking the heroine and hero from danger to enduring love and happy-ever-after is all in a day's work for her, and who could complain about a day like that?

Books by Joanna Wayne

HARLEQUIN INTRIGUE

*Randolph Family Ties

Don't miss any of our special offers. Write to us at the following address for information on our newest releases.

Harlequin Reader Service
U.S.: 3010 Walden Ave., P.O. Box 1325, Buffalo, NY 14269
Canadian: P.O. Box 609, Fort Erie, Ont. L2A 5X3

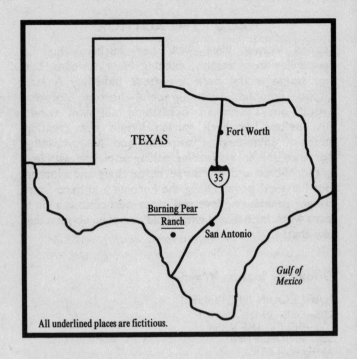

TEXAS

Fort Worth

35

Burning Pear
Ranch

San Antonio

Gulf of
Mexico

All underlined places are fictitious.

CAST OF CHARACTERS

Ryder Randolph—The youngest of the Randolph brothers. He'd do anything to keep his child out of danger.

Kathi Sable—She'll do anything to protect her baby girl, even walk away from the only man she's ever loved.

Dillon, Branson and Langley Randolph— Ryder Randolph's brothers, each with his own concerns about the woman who has walked back into Ryder's life.

Mary Randolph—Ryder's mom and the adoring grandmother of his daughter, Betsy.

Arlo Camionos—A retired Texas Ranger who still maintains contact with a lot of men in high and low places.

Shawn Priest—A friend of Ryder Randolph. When his body is found on the Burning Pear Ranch, Ryder must uncover a host of deadly secrets.

Julia Rodrigue—She was Shawn's friend, but is she lying when she claims she knows nothing about his murder?

Bull Ruffkins—A friend of Shawn Priest's. If he knows who the murderer is, he's not talking.

Peyton Ferran—Julia Rodrigue's husband. He's rich enough to give Julia everything money can buy.

Kent Quay—A Fort Worth policeman with secrets of his own.

Joshua Kincaid—He owns a string of Texas-themed nightclubs called Kincaid's. He was Kathi's boss until fear forced her to run.

To women everywhere who love reading
about tough, sexy Texas cowboys.
Hope the Randolph brothers find a place
in your heart.

And to Wayne, always.

Prologue

The weathered cowboy killed the bulldozer's engine. Lifting his hat from his mussed hair, he wiped his sleeve across his forehead and then glanced upward. He'd been at this for half a day and he was tired and drier than the middle of a haystack.

Luckily he had a six-pack of colas iced down in the cooler he kept in the back of his pickup. He stretched out of the uncomfortable seat, stepped onto the fender, and jumped to the ground.

Stepping gingerly, he crossed a few feet of the freshly upturned soil. His boots scraped against the broken mesquite roots as his heels ground into the loose, pungent earth. It was amazing how the maze of roots could grow so thick. That's why every dozen or so years, someone had to come in with a 'dozer and turn it all under, killing the brush and giving the grass a fair shot at providing a decent pasture.

It was hard work, but he was glad to get the job. The Randolphs were good to work for. They treated a hand fair and paid on time. The wind picked up and he blinked as the dust whirled and flew into his eyes. Turning, he kicked at a gnarled piece of twisted root that had become entangled with his boot.

Something caught his eye. He hunched over and knocked a clump of dirt from a strange-looking root. His hands grew clammy. This wasn't a root at all. He dug around some more, his throat growing so tight it was hard to swallow.

A second later, he stood and rushed to his truck. Reaching inside, he grabbed the cell phone and punched in the number for the sheriff's office.

"Sheriff Randolph here."

"Branson, this is Max Crete."

"You sound upset, Max. What's up?"

"I'm out at the Burning Pear doing some work for your brother Langley. I think you need to come out here."

"If you've got a problem, why don't you call Langley? He's probably a lot closer than I am."

"No, Sheriff, I called the right man, and I think you oughta make it quick. I just dug up a body, or at least what's left of it."

Chapter One

One week later...

Kathi Sable opened the front door of her small rented house and scanned the street before stepping onto the porch. The precaution was one of the many habits she'd entrenched in her daily routine.

It was a rule of survival, like her frequent moves and name changes. In this town, she was Susan Campbell, a redhead from Williamsburg, Virginia, who'd moved to Mobile, Alabama, to find work. She handled the office duties for a small construction firm. The boss was great. He asked few questions and didn't give a ding about her past or her private life. He was far too busy trying to keep his wife and his girlfriend happy.

A beige Ford sedan turned the corner and drove slowly down her street. She stepped back inside the door until it passed, but filed away the color and make in her mind. She couldn't be too careful.

When the coast was clear, she hurried down the steps and bent to pick up her morning paper. The garage door across the street hummed open and Mr.

Scrivener backed down his driveway in his gray minivan. She waved and smiled, playing the part of the nice single neighbor who lived alone and didn't bother anyone.

The role wasn't all that difficult. After all, she'd had almost two years' practice and with lots of different neighbors. The names changed. Everything else stayed the same.

Only she liked this street and this house—and she loved Mobile. It had a slow, southern pulse to it, a rhythm that eased some of the pressure she'd come to expect from just being alive. The people were nice, too. She could have made friends easily if she'd been free to do so. But she spent her time alone.

Always alone. It was the ties to other people that tripped her up, made her vulnerable. For once in her life, she was even thankful that she had no family to drag into this.

Her dad and stepsisters lived on another continent and probably wouldn't have noticed she'd gone missing even if they'd lived in the same state. They'd stopped keeping in touch years before.

Stepping back inside the confines of her cozy house, she padded down the hall and into the kitchen. The odor of freshly brewed coffee wafted through the air, and she breathed deeply, absorbing the comforting aroma. Stepping to the counter, she poured her first cup while she glanced at the morning headlines.

A local politician convicted of fraud. Floods in the low-lying areas of the city. A major pileup that claimed five lives in Georgia.

She took a sip of the coffee and then walked to

the table so that she had enough room to spread out her paper. The inside articles were her favorite. Occasionally there was something about her home state of Texas, the closest thing she ever got to a letter from home.

She scanned the pages, pausing to read an article on day care centers and one on a boy who'd saved his friend from drowning in a freak boating accident. And then her eyes slid to the bottom corner.

Ryder Randolph, the youngest brother of Senator Dillon Randolph, has been questioned about the murder of his one-time friend Shawn Priest.

The breath rushed from her lungs, and her hands trembled so that the hot liquid spilled over the rim of the mug and slid onto her fingers. She was only distantly aware of the burn.

Kathi finished the article and then read it one more time before pushing the newspaper aside. She'd never thought it would come to this. But it had.

Standing, she walked to the window and peered out into the side yard. Her tulips were in full bloom, brilliant blossoms that brushed away the weariness of winter. The dogwood tree in the corner of her backyard was white with tiny cross-shaped blossoms that promised life was starting again.

Only the promises were lies. It was danger that was starting again. Danger and heartbreak, and a past that would never let go. Only she had to make it end. If not for herself, than for Ryder and for their daughter.

Betsy. Her Betsy. Suddenly her arms ached with a pain so intense she could barely stand the weight of them.

Her bare feet padded across the cool kitchen floor as she hurried to her bedroom to pack. She had no choice but to step out of the shadows.

Even if it meant facing a killer.

Chapter Two

Ryder sat in the sheriff's office. He'd been in here a hundred times before, but it had always been to visit his brother Branson. But it wasn't Branson sitting across from him today. It was Grover Brown, a Texas Ranger who'd taken over when Branson had been relieved of his authority in Shawn Priest's murder case.

A man was not expected to investigate a murder in which his brother was a suspect. Of course, it wasn't usually the Texas Rangers who came in to help out. But this case was bigger than most. Ryder's brother Dillon was a Texas state senator with a lot of clout.

Hard on crime. Hard on criminals. Keep the great state of Texas safe. That had been Dillon's campaign promise. Now his brother was wanted for murder. The papers were having a field day.

Grover leaned forward in his chair. "I appreciate your coming in willingly, Ryder. It makes it a lot easier when someone works with us."

"I'm trying to cooperate. The media makes it a little difficult. I say I had nothing to do with the murder. They twist it around, and it sounds like I just confessed to the crime.''

''I'm not here to twist things around or to get a headline,'' Grover said, punctuating his words with a smile. ''All I'm looking for is facts.''

''The facts are simple.'' Ryder crossed a booted foot over his knee. ''I don't have a clue as to how Shawn's body ended up at the Burning Pear. As far as I know, he'd never even been to our ranch when he was alive.''

''But you did know Shawn?''

''Not all that well, but I called him a friend. I never had any reason not to. I met him when he started hanging around at the rodeo grounds while we were practicing. Later we got to know each other pretty good. We went to dinner, out for a beer or two, that sort of thing.''

''According to what I have on Shawn Priest, his last known place of employment was Kincaid's. That's a chain of Texas-themed nightclubs that operate around the state. He worked in the Fort Worth club.''

''That's where he worked when I knew him. I'm not sure what he did. I guess you'd have to ask Joshua Kincaid that.''

''Don't worry. We'll be talking to Mr. Kincaid. We'll be talking to everyone Shawn worked with, unless something shows up soon to point in one way or another.'' Grover scratched a spot over his left temple, as if he were deep in thought. ''Do you know any reason why someone would have wanted to kill Shawn Priest?''

Ryder shook his head. He'd asked himself that

same question many times over the past week. He'd never come up with any satisfying answers. Just a few speculations. "I don't know why anyone would want to kill Shawn, but there were some people he didn't see eye-to-eye with."

"Could you tell me about them?"

"I can't tell you much. I don't know much. I know he was talking about quitting his job because he was having problems with his boss."

"Would that be the personnel manager at Kincaid's?"

"No, that would be Mr. Kincaid himself. I can't say for sure what was eating Shawn, but he was aggravated with Joshua Kincaid. I assume it was job-related."

"Who else was he having problems with?"

"His fiancée had broken off his engagement. He was upset with her. I guess she was probably more upset with him. She told him not to call her anymore."

"Anyone else?"

"Not that I can think of."

"And you and Shawn had no arguments."

"I didn't say that. We argued over a lot of things. Who was going to win the Pennant race. Who was the best roper on the circuit. Were the Dallas Cowboys going to have a good year. That kind of stuff, but it was all friendly."

"And when was the last time you saw Shawn Priest alive?"

Ryder rubbed his hands together. "You know I told all of this to someone else the other day. I'm sure he has a record of my answers."

"I'm sure he does, but I've been asked to coordinate the investigation, and I get a better feel when I question a suspect myself."

What he meant was, a better chance to catch the guy he was interrogating in a lie. But he could question him every day for the next twenty years. Ryder didn't lie, not to anyone. Honesty was the mark of a real man, and it was expected in the Randolph household. He'd learned that lesson at a young age, both at and over his dad's knee.

"I'm not sure of the date I last saw Shawn, but it was a few days before I was plowed into by a hit-and-run driver. My knee was busted up, and I left the rodeo circuit to come home for treatment. That was nearly two years ago."

"And everything was fine with Shawn at that time?"

"No, it wasn't fine. He'd made up his mind to quit his job. He didn't know where he was going to look for more work or even what he wanted to do, other than that he wanted a change. He even talked about training for the rodeo, but I think that was just talk."

The questioning went on and on. Covering the same ground as the last time he'd talked. Only then the body had just been found, and Ryder had stupidly thought the questioning was just routine. The newspaper and television reporters had made it clear that wasn't the case. Ryder Randolph was a major suspect in the murder of his one-time friend, Shawn Priest.

To tell the truth, he wished now he'd never met the guy. But if he'd never met Shawn, he'd never have met Kathi Sable...and he would never have had his beautiful daughter.

Finally Grover decided he'd covered enough ground. Ryder left before he changed his mind. He'd been cooped up in this cube of a room for far too long. He got claustrophobic when he was closed in. He needed fresh air to breathe, room to stretch.

He needed a beer.

KATHI PULLED into the parking lot of Kelman's only real nightspot just as the sun started to set. It had been a long drive from Mobile to this town tucked away in the isolated flatlands of south Texas. She'd grabbed a few hours' sleep last night in an inexpensive motel. The rest of the time she'd been on the road, stopping only to eat and fill her tank with gas.

A few miles back, her neck and shoulder muscles had ached and her eyes had been heavy with sleep. But once she'd spotted the Welcome to Kelman sign, anxiety washed away the fatigue. By the time she'd stopped at the pay phone to call the Randolph ranch, her heart had been beating faster than the sticks of a hard-rock drummer. It still was.

Her hands gripped the wheel much too tightly as she scanned the area. More than a dozen vehicles were parked in the Roadhouse lot, most of them pickup trucks. If Ryder Randolph was here as his mom had said, she should be able to find him easily enough. She snaked between the parked cars until she spotted his truck, the same red Ford he'd had when they'd dated in Fort Worth. Her breath caught in her throat. Her hands grew shaky.

It had been nearly two years since she'd seen Ryder, but not a day had gone by that she hadn't thought of him. Not a night that she hadn't snuggled under the covers and wished he were there beside her. Now she had to walk up to him and pretend she hadn't missed him at all. Sucking in a shaky breath, she opened the door of her car and stepped out onto the asphalt pavement.

RYDER RANDOLPH wrapped his fingers around the long neck of a cold beer. He'd come here to escape, but it wasn't working. His mind couldn't seem to leave the problems behind.

Cops, jail, murder. The words and images passed through his mind and then disappeared. His three brothers were going in circles, arguing about how to handle his defense if he was officially accused. Dillon had already called in some big-gun lawyer from the West Coast to represent him, but Ryder was still having trouble gearing up for a fight he never expected to face. He was innocent, so how could they find any real evidence to use against him?

What he couldn't get away from was the fact that someone had killed Shawn Priest and buried him at the Burning Pear. The murderer surely hadn't chosen that spot by accident. As far as Ryder knew, Shawn had never even been to this part of Texas.

He took another sip of the beer and then looked up as the door opened and a young woman walked into the smoky bar. It was seldom that someone he didn't know stopped in the Roadhouse, but this woman was the exception. She scanned the room tentatively and then fixed her stare on him.

Irritation grated along his nerves. If she was a reporter looking for a scoop, she could carry her pad and pen somewhere else. He had nothing to say.

Turning, he diverted his gaze to a group of cowboys at the bar. When he finally looked back in her direction, she was still staring. Nervy—he'd give her that. But that was the way those news babes were, or so he'd heard. This one looked familiar. He might have seen her on some news show when he'd been on the road.

She might have even interviewed him when he'd been king of the suicide circuit, riding broncs to the top of the rodeo rung on the way to his famed silver buckle. But, it wasn't the bronc rider she'd be interested in tonight. Standing, he downed his beer and set the empty bottle back on the table.

The woman joined him before he could duck out. "Hello, Ryder."

The voice cut into his composure. It was too familiar, too seductive. A voice from his past? He studied her face.

"You don't recognize me, do you?"

"I can't say that I do."

"I'm Kathi Sable."

He blinked and swallowed hard. But the woman standing in front of him was not the Kathi Sable from his past. This woman's hair was dark and thick. Kathi's had been fine, the color of wheat, the consistency of silk. This woman wore thick layers of makeup. Kathi had worn almost none. Her skin had been baby-soft, her lips full and rich. No one changed that much, that fast.

"If this is your idea of a joke, lady, I don't find it a damn bit funny."

She took off her glasses and laid them on the table. Her gaze locked with his, and in that split second, he knew that the woman in front of him was no imposter. His heart dropped to his stomach and her name slipped from his lips. "Kathi."

Her fingers tangled in the thick locks of dark hair that fell about her face. "I need to talk to you, Ryder." She looked around the room nervously and then turned her gaze back to him. "Can we go somewhere quieter? Somewhere we can be alone?"

He nodded, his mind playing cruel tricks on him, making him remember things better forgotten. He hadn't seen or heard from Kathi in almost two years. Not a phone call. Not a card. Nothing but the baby girl she'd had someone else deliver to his door.

Now she was back, just as unexpectedly as she'd left. That could only mean one thing. "Is this about Betsy?"

"Why?" She nailed him with a piercing stare. "She's all right, isn't she?"

"She's fine. Motherless, but fine all the same." He hadn't meant to sound so accusatory, but resentment had swelled up too fast to combat it.

Kathi scanned the room again and then turned back to him. "I have to get out of here, Ryder. Name a place we can talk in private. I'll meet you there."

"We could go to the ranch. Mom and my brother Branson and his wife will be around, but the house is big enough we can talk without being disturbed." He played with the empty beer bottle, rocking it back and forth.

She blinked and bit her bottom lip. "No. I can't go there."

"Just as well. *Our* daughter is sleeping. I'm sure you wouldn't want to disturb her, especially since you haven't bothered to visit or even call to ask about her since you deserted her."

"Please, Ryder." Her voice shook on the words, and he strained to hear her above the jukebox. "Don't make this any harder for me than it already is."

Moisture glazed her eyes, and Ryder glimpsed a depth of pain that caught him off guard. Reacting on impulse, he reached for her hand. She jerked it away. The rejection hit like a sucker punch below the belt. He pushed it aside, amazed she still had the power to hurt him after all this time.

"We could go to Gus's Café," he said, suddenly anxious to hear what she had to say and get her out of his life again. "You probably saw it if you came through town."

"I saw it. There were several cars parked in front. I'd rather go somewhere *totally* private." She clasped her hands about the strap of her shoulder bag. "I know you have reason to be resentful, Ryder, but what I have to say to you is important."

Impulsively, his hands knotted into hard fists. "I'm listening."

She stood. "I can't talk here. Tell me where to meet you. Then wait at least five minutes before you follow. It's best if no one thinks we're leaving together."

"So that's the way it is now." He grabbed his jacket from the back of the chair. "Drive out of the parking lot and take a left. There's a crossroad a half mile down. Turn left there and go to the first turnoff.

There's a gate, but it's not locked. Unlatch it and drive through.''

''Where will that take me?''

''The land belongs to us now, but it was a camping area before we bought it. There are still some picnic tables down by the creek. We can sit and talk and have all the privacy you want.''

She turned without saying a word and walked away. Her hips hadn't lost the sensual sway that had turned him on the first time he'd seen her. It still affected him. Only there were so many feelings churning inside him right now, he'd be hard-pressed to name any one of them.

The hands on his watch moved in slow motion as he waited for the prescribed five minutes to tick off. His insides were shaky, and his brain wasn't exactly running on all cylinders. Not that he had ever been a rocket scientist where Kathi Sable was concerned.

He'd proven that the night he'd met her. The Fort Worth rodeo grounds had been packed. Lots of points had been up for grabs, and that always brought out the top competitors and the crowds. He'd just finished the night's bronc-riding competition and was strutting around, reveling in his success.

As always, his new buddy Shawn Priest was waiting for him, but that night he hadn't come alone. He'd brought Kathi out for her first taste of rodeo. Excited, bubbly, sexy beyond belief, she'd impressed the hell out of Ryder.

The three of them went out for a late-night steak and a couple of beers, and Ryder reminded himself over and over that she was off-limits. He didn't hit on his friend's dates.

The next day *she* had called and asked *him* out. When he hesitated, she'd insisted she and Shawn were nothing more than friends. Still, he'd called Shawn to make sure he saw things the same way. Whether he did or not, Shawn had given him the go-ahead to date Kathi.

He'd gone to her place to pick her up for dinner. He'd stayed for breakfast. And once they'd made love, he couldn't get enough—not that night, or any other, during the glorious two weeks that followed. Amazingly enough, his performance in the arenas had never been better. He was riding on the top of the world, but the ride had been short and the fall had been the worst of his life.

From the heights to the depths in one split second. One car spinning out of control. One hit-and-run. He'd wound up in the hospital. Kathi had just wound up gone.

No glory. No woman. A rodeo story as old as the sport itself.

Now Kathi was back, and it was obviously not because she wanted to take up where they'd left off. If she was coming here thinking she'd just waltz in after more than a year and take their daughter away from him, she was just plain nuts.

Five minutes or not, he wasn't waiting around any longer. Tugging his Stetson low over his forehead, he strolled out the door.

And to yet another bit of bad news. The front tire on his truck was as flat as a raw tortilla.

THE SUN had disappeared completely and the moon shone in the sky by the time Kathi turned off on the dirt road that Ryder had told her to take. The gate was there, just as he'd said it would be. She stopped her car, opened the door and stepped out.

A noise startled her. She froze to the spot, her heart slamming against her chest until she spotted the armadillo. The small mammal scratched at the ground, his chunky armor catching the glint of moonlight. Perfectly harmless, but it didn't take much to send her into a panic attack these days.

Reaching over the top of the wooden railing, she unlatched the gate and swung it open. It creaked and whined in protest, but it moved easily.

Once the gate was open, she climbed back in her car and drove through it. She stopped, about to get out and close the gate behind her when she spotted the glow of headlights bouncing off the dirt road and the scrubby brush that bordered parts of the fence line. Either Ryder hadn't waited the five minutes she'd asked him to or else he'd driven with his accelerator on the floorboard. She drove on, leaving the gate open for him.

Ryder Randolph, cowboy extraordinaire. She'd recognized him the instant she'd located him in the back of the Roadhouse, but he had changed. He looked older. And even when he'd finally realized it was her, he hadn't broken into the familiar boyish grin that used to propel her heart into double time.

Ryder was different. She was different. And ugly secrets had built a wall between them. Still, in a few moments she'd be alone with him. Just the two of them, sitting by the creek in the darkness. They'd done that before. Her body heated up as old memories crashed her mind. She struggled to push the erotic imagery aside.

The past was over.

Suck it up and face the music, Kathi Sable. Ryder Randolph may own a white horse, but he is not going to ride in on it and save you. No one can.

She turned her attention back to steering the car as the road circled a cluster of picnic tables. She peered past them, to a dribble of water that ran through a creek bed that was half-dry. But it met the criteria. It was moving and it was wet, at least it was now.

She lowered her foot on the brake pedal, then yanked the gearshift into park and killed the engine. An owl hooted as she stepped from the car. "So you don't like company trespassing on your hunting grounds? Don't worry, I won't be here long."

Evidently he didn't take her at her word. He spread his wings and flew to another patch of mesquite a little closer to the water. She followed, making her way slowly through the tall grass.

She'd almost reached the edge of the creek when she saw the glow from Ryder's headlights. His truck slowed and then stopped as it reached her car. But when the driver stepped out, she could tell at once that it wasn't Ryder.

Panic knotted in her stomach, hard and cold, as the man stalked over to her car, waving a powerful flashlight. Somehow she managed to move, ducking behind a clump of brush as the beam of the flashlight left her car and swept the area around her.

Barely daring to breathe, she waited until the light veered off in another direction. Then, as stealthy as a snake, she crept through the grass and toward the water. But the beam of light returned. She rolled away, but not quickly enough.

A volley of gunfire shattered the quiet. She slid into the water. Her ankle caught on something, and she wrenched it free, as another round of shots went off and a shower of bullets sprayed the muddy bank. She stayed under the shallow ribbon of murky water as long as she could, forcing her muscles to project her through the numbing cold.

She surfaced a few yards downstream. Using her arms, she pulled her body to the soft earth and then rolled away from the water's edge before trying to stand. Excruciating pain shot up her leg and forced her back to the ground. Silently cursing her fate, she rolled under a thorny bush and waited.

Time moved in strange circles, fading in and out. The grass and brush rustled with movement. The wind, nocturnal creatures, monsters.

A vicious shudder shook her wet body. Someone was coming. She could hear his footsteps and see the ever-widening arc of his flashlight's beam.

She worked her hands into the pocket of her damp jeans and pulled out the only weapon she had. A lousy pocketknife, but it would have to do. Holding the exposed point in front of her, she waited until the hand touched her leg. Then, adrenaline surging like blood through an open artery, she swung her arm and struck.

Chapter Three

Ryder jerked back. Dodging vicious kicks, he grabbed the slim wrist that held the thrusting knife and pulled Kathi from beneath a tangle of thorny brush.

"Ryder, it's you. Thank goodness!"

"Now that's what I call a welcome." His words were punctuated by air rushing from his lungs in relief as he ran the beam of his light across her body. The term "rode hard and put away wet" had never seemed a better fit, but she was alive and kicking and her pulse beneath his fingers was strong and fast. "Are you all right?"

"I've been better."

"You've looked better." He let go of her wrist. A million questions bucked in his mind, all centered around the fact that Kathi Sable had stepped back into his life. Now, he'd found her scared and cowering, like a rabbit hiding from a hungry coyote. Fortunately the coyote had missed his meal.

He took a clean handkerchief from his back pocket and dabbed at a smear of mud on her forehead. "Do you want to tell me what's going on here?"

She scanned the area and then turned back to him. "It's a long story."

"I don't doubt it, but I'll bet it's fascinating."

"More bizarre than fascinating." She shivered and hugged her arms around her drenched body. "Someone followed me here. At first I thought it was you." She looked around again, as if she expected the man to materialize from the darkness.

"You can relax," he assured her. "Whoever it was is gone. Evidently he saw my headlights when I turned in and hightailed it out of here. When he passed me he was little more than an engine roar and a cloud of dust." He hunched down beside her and looked her in the eye. "Who was he?"

"I have no idea."

"Why do I have trouble buying that?"

"I guess you're just a suspicious sort."

"Yeah. It couldn't be because you showed up in Kelman acting like a reenactment from *Unsolved Mysteries?* Or because now I find you hiding and trembling with fear?"

"I hid because I thought I was in danger. I'm not denying that. I hid well, too. *He* didn't find me, so how did *you?*"

"I'm good." And because thankfully he'd learned tracking from a ranger who knew this area like the back of his hand. The wind picked up, and Ryder unbuttoned his jacket, shrugged out of it and threw it over Kathi's shoulders. It wouldn't do much toward keeping her warm, but it was the best he had to offer.

She hugged it around her like a cloak and then took Ryder's arm. "We have to get out of here."

Her voice was shaky, but her grip was strong. Throwing her weight against him, she struggled to stand. He caught her as she yelped in pain and doubled over.

"It's my ankle," she said. "My foot caught on something as I slid into the water."

Ryder leaned over her, shining the beam of his flashlight on the ankle that was already swollen to twice its size. "You can't walk on that."

"I'm not staying out here." Her muscles strained as she rocked forward and put a little weight on her foot. This time her squeal was a good imitation of a mouse with its tail caught in a trap.

"If you were a horse, I'd have to shoot you," he joked, though the gruff strain in his voice killed his feeble attempt at humor. There was nothing funny about the woman from his past who sat groaning at his feet. Nothing funny about the situation, or the fact that she was undoubtedly in deep trouble.

"Just help me back to my car, Ryder. It was a mistake to come here. I know that now. I'll leave and you can pretend tonight never happened."

"And miss hearing your fascinating story? I don't think so." He reached down and lifted her into his arms, throwing her over his shoulder like a sack of feed.

Actually, she wasn't much heavier than a sack of feed, but the shape was entirely different. Old memories reared up in his mind as her body pressed against his, images of the two weeks of passion they'd shared so long ago. He pushed them aside. The cold, hard reality of the present was all that was left of what they'd shared.

Reality and their daughter.

He forced his mind to focus on the inconsistencies as he started up the muddy incline and then across the flat grassland to the spot where he'd left his truck. "So now that a talk by the creek is out, where would you like to finish this conversation?"

"Do yourself a favor, Ryder. Ride off into the sunset alone. Believe me, you're better off not knowing anything more."

"It's too late for that. The sun's already set." He reached the narrow dirt road and headed toward his truck, walking a little faster now that he knew where he was planting his feet. "I'll drive. We'll come back for your car later."

"I can't just leave it out here," she protested, jerking her head around.

"Sure you can. It's not in anybody's way. And I doubt very seriously the man you're running from is after your car." He placed her down gingerly next to his truck.

"I never said I was running from anyone."

"You didn't have to. I may look like a dumb cowboy. I'm not one."

"Then don't jump to conclusions. I'm sure the man who attacked me just noticed that I was alone. When I turned onto a dark, country road, he followed."

"Yeah, right. The man was just driving around Kelman, Texas, looking for a woman to attack. That's about as likely as your traveling incognito just for the fun of it." He reached over and tugged the dark wig back from her forehead. Blond locks escaped to fall over her eyes. He brushed them away and then reeled as an unexpected jolt of longing hit.

"Your disguise is good, though," he said, when he was sure his voice wouldn't give him away. "I had a hard time believing it was you back at the Roadhouse, even after you told me." He yanked the truck door open.

"Okay, Ryder. I am running from someone. But it's my problem, and you can get a much better story from any novel on the bookshelf. So why don't I just get back in my car and disappear from your life again?"

"Bad idea. You're wet and shivering and injured."

"I'll be fine. The car has a heater and it's my left ankle that's hurt. It won't affect my driving."

"I don't think so, Kathi. I get very disappointed when someone promises me an intriguing story and then backs out."

"Fine. We'll talk here, and then you can be on your way in a few minutes."

"I thought you said this was a *long* story."

"I talk fast."

And in crazy circles. But, if he had any sense, he'd probably do as she'd asked—deposit her at her car and walk away. Only he couldn't. She was in trouble and no matter how he felt about her, no matter what she'd done, she was still the mother of his child. That had to count for something.

He half lifted, half guided her through the passenger door of his pickup and onto the seat. "We tried your way once, why not try it my way now? The

Burning Pear is just a few miles from here. We can talk there and tend to your ankle.''

He was crazy. He was sure of it. Betsy was the only possible explanation for why Kathi had marched back into his life after all this time.

He couldn't keep Kathi from seeing Betsy, even if he wanted to, which he didn't. Betsy needed her mother in her life. But he damn well wasn't going to turn his baby girl over to a woman who ran around the country in disguise, playing hide-and-seek with some kind of stalker. So why was he inviting the woman into his home?

Kathi laid her right hand on Ryder's arm. ''I can't go to the Burning Pear, Ryder.'' She splayed her other hand across her chest, as if she were holding her heart in place. ''Any place but there.''

''Fine by me. Just remember, you made the call.'' Evidently he could forget his concerns about Kathi wanting to take Betsy from him. If she didn't so much as want to see Betsy, surely she didn't want to get custody of her.

''Do you need anything from your car?''

''My jacket. It's in the trunk.'' She handed him the key.

He got the jacket and the couple of pieces of worn luggage next to it. She'd need dry clothes.

''Buckle up,'' he said, once he'd returned to the truck and climbed behind the wheel. He turned the key in the ignition and jerked the truck into gear. ''This ride will be a little rough.''

''Is there any other kind?''

KATHI WINCED with each bounce of the truck down the rutted dirt road. Her ankle throbbed, her head ached, and her heart was crumbling into tiny pieces.

Yesterday coming to Kelman had seemed her only choice. Tonight she knew it had been a huge mistake. She had come here thinking she could help Ryder, but all she had really done was drag him into the deadly secrets she lived with every day.

She stretched and tried to move her foot. A pain stabbed her lower leg. She bit back the groan, leaving it to rattle inside her. But apparently Ryder read the agony anyway.

"Hang on for a few more minutes, and we'll get some ice for that ankle."

"It'll be all right."

"It'll be better with ice. You can prop it up while we're talking. That should help some, too."

"Where are we going?"

"To a ranch that belongs to a friend of mine. Arlo Camionos."

"That's not a good idea, Ryder, not under the present circumstances. I don't want to cause trouble for anyone."

"It's a little late for that. But don't waste your energy worrying about Arlo. I'd match him up against a pack of wild jackals."

And that still might not put him in the league of what she had to offer. But no need to mention that to Ryder. After what happened at the creek a few minutes ago, she knew she couldn't tell him what she'd come here to say. If she did, he'd never let her walk away.

"So what does Arlo do that makes him so tough?"

she asked, as Ryder dodged a tumbleweed that cart-wheeled across the road in front of them.

"He spends his days working cattle now, but up until a couple of years ago he was one of the fiercest Texas Rangers around."

"What happened two years ago? Did he retire?"

"More like an honorable discharge. He took a bullet in the left hand, and it was either a desk job or home to the ranch. He chose the ranch."

The gate was open when they got to Arlo's spread. Ryder drove through and then stopped. "Arlo was one of the few who could empathize when I thought I'd have to give up the rodeo to a senseless injury." He stepped out of the truck and walked over to close and latch the gate.

Shifting in her seat, she studied his profile. He was as handsome as ever, but he'd lost much of the boyish enthusiasm for life that she'd found so exciting when they'd first met. Or maybe he hadn't lost it at all. It could be that being questioned as a suspect in a murder case had dulled it. Or maybe it was seeing her again that had brought him down.

If so, the change was understandable. The two weeks they'd dated had been all cotton candy and roller coasters, as exciting as a child's first trip to the midway at the State Fair. She'd been crazy about him, couldn't wait to see him, hated it when he left.

And then she'd walked away without explanation, left town the same day she'd watched Ryder bounce off the front fender of a plain, black sedan and crash to the hard pavement.

The image was embedded in her brain. Cold, hard, ugly. She'd pulled up the picture time after time, replaying it as she might a haunting old video. The remembered scene chilled and poisoned, but it kept her on her toes, made her ever aware that danger was all she had to offer to Ryder or their daughter.

She'd heeded the warning well—until yesterday. Now she'd have to run again. A new name. A new job. A new city.

Only the heartbreak and fear would remain the same.

KATHI SAT on the nubby green sofa in Arlo's narrow, high-ceilinged living room, wrapped in a heavy blanket, her foot propped on pillows that had been arranged on a low coffee table. The furnishings were sparse, well-worn, functional. The wooden floor was clean, but dull and marred, and the only illumination came from a bare lightbulb hanging from the ceiling.

The house smelled of smoke and burned wood, though the ashes in the stone fireplace were cold tonight. Glassy eyes stared from the antlered head mounted over the heavy oak mantel. She stared back for a moment and then shifted her gaze downward, to the pine coffee table and the stack of newspapers that rested next to her injured ankle.

The room lacked the cozy touches a woman might have added, but it reeked of the man who lived there. Arlo Camionos was larger than life, at least six foot six, with a full beard just beginning to gray and eyes that burned as if they were backlit by a fiery torch.

Ryder had volunteered little explanation when they'd arrived, only that she was a friend of his who he'd run into at the Roadhouse. They'd gone down by the creek at the old Larker campground to walk and talk of old times, but she'd sprained her ankle. They'd come here for first aid rather than wake up his mom and daughter.

Apparently Arlo and Ryder were close. The retired ranger hadn't looked at all surprised to see Ryder at his door with a strange woman, but his expression had changed the second Ryder had said her name.

Arlo stood a few feet away now, studying her while Ryder raided the refrigerator for ice for her ankle. "Do you plan to stay in Kelman long?" he asked, his gaze never leaving her face.

"No, I'm just passing through."

"Then you didn't come here specifically to see Ryder?"

"No." She shifted uncomfortably and averted her gaze.

"Too bad about the sprain," he said, stepping over to get a better view of the swollen flesh. "But lucky that you ran into Ryder. Or do you have a lot of old friends around Kelman?"

He was baiting her, digging for information. He might not be a ranger any longer, but apparently he hadn't lost his intuitive feel for spotting trouble or his lawman's ability to recognize a lie.

"I didn't just run into Ryder," she said, meeting the man's steely gaze. "I called his house and his mother told me where I could find him."

"Did you tell Mrs. Randolph that you were Betsy's mother?"

The question caught her off guard, but it answered one of her silent questions. He apparently knew all about her. "All I told Mrs. Randolph was that I was a friend of Ryder's and wanted to talk to him."

She looked up thankfully as Ryder stepped back into the room carrying a thin green towel and a plastic zip-bag full of ice cubes. He crossed the room, folding the towel around the makeshift ice bag as he approached. He bent and fitted it to her painful ankle.

"That should slow down the swelling," he said. He turned to Arlo. "Have you got any painkillers? Even the over-the-counter variety would help."

"I've got bourbon," he said. "It's the best painkiller I know of."

Kathi leaned forward and readjusted the ice pack, tucking the towel around her ankle so that it held the bag in place. "Bourbon would be great," she said. "Straight up."

Arlo went for the drink. Ryder rearranged the pillows he'd stuffed behind her back. His hands were sure, yet gentle. She trembled as her mind left the risky confines of this room and pictured him holding their baby girl.

The image wasn't new. She woke with it on busy mornings, went to bed with it on lonely nights. But the image had become fuzzy over the past few months. The infant she'd held in her arms just after she'd given birth wasn't an infant any longer. Betsy's first birthday was sneaking up fast, and try as she might, Kathi couldn't picture her baby as a toddler.

She hadn't seen her daughter creep, hadn't heard her first words, hadn't been there when she'd started pulling up to cruise the furniture. The loss was all-pervasive. Now there was only a heartbreaking gap where the memories should have lived.

Arlo returned with her drink and set the short glass on the coffee table. "There's plenty more if you need it.'' He turned his attention back to Ryder. "I'm going to turn in now, but you're welcome to the bourbon or anything else around here. You know where everything is.''

Ryder nodded. "Would you mind if Kathi used one of your spare bedrooms tonight?''

Arlo stared at Kathi, his expression shouting his reluctance to get involved. Smart man. But after a few seconds hesitation, he hooked his thumbs into the corners of his front pockets and managed a slight smile. *"Mi casa, su casa.* The sheets are clean, and there are extra towels hanging in the bathroom.''

"I appreciate the offer,'' she said, "but I won't be staying. I have previous commitments that require me to be in San Antonio by morning.''

"Whatever,'' he said, stroking his beard. "The offer still stands.'' Arlo started to leave, but stopped at the entrance to the narrow hallway and turned back to face them. "If you need me, Ryder, you know where I'll be. Otherwise just let yourselves out when you've finished talking.''

"Will do, Arlo. And I know what Kathi said, but her ankle's worse than she wants to admit. Don't be surprised if she's still here when you wake up in the morning.''

"Whether she is or not, why don't you give me a call in the a.m., Ryder. I have a couple of ideas to kick around with you.''

Kathi waited until Arlo's retreating footsteps faded to silence before reaching for the glass of bourbon. She touched it to her lips and sipped the amber liquid. It slid down her throat in a stinging burn.

It was the first time she'd drunk anything stronger

than wine or an occasional beer since… She shuddered as the all-too-familiar image darkened her mind.

She leaned forward. "I read about you being questioned in the death of Shawn Priest."

"So that's what brought you back after all these months." The muscles in his face tightened and his eyes narrowed. "I didn't kill him."

"I know."

"Too bad the cops don't share that theory." He pulled a slat-backed wooden chair close to the couch and then straddled it, folding his arms over the top rail. "Did you see Shawn again after my accident?"

"No."

Ryder frowned. "Neither did I. I just wonder if things would have turned out differently for him if I hadn't gotten hurt when I did. He'd talked about wanting to go the rodeo route, though he didn't know that much about riding. I think he was just looking for a change."

"I think he was in some kind of trouble." She had to be careful. Weigh her words. Give nothing away. The best thing she could do for Ryder and for Betsy was to just disappear. "Shawn had made a hero out of you. He wouldn't have just walked away without a very good reason."

Ryder's eyes shadowed. "I wouldn't bet on that. Walking away didn't seem to bother you, and I thought we were very close at the time."

Regret balled in Kathi's stomach. "It wasn't like that."

"Wasn't it?" Ryder stood, his eyes dark pools of condemnation. "But I don't blame you, Kathi. What good is a rodeo contender who's laid up with a bum knee?'' He stepped closer, towering over her. ''I can understand your deciding to discard our relationship, Kathi, but tell me, how did you come to the conclusion that your daughter was disposable, as well?''

Anger rose inside her, merging and mixing with the regret until she could barely hold back the words of denial that burned in her throat. Ryder had no right to hurl accusations, not after what she'd been through. But how could she blame him when he had no clue as to what had really come between them?

She struggled to present a calm front despite the storm of hurt that raged inside her. ''I didn't throw away our daughter, Ryder. I got her to you. You had everything to offer her. I had nothing.''

He paced the room and turned to level her with an accusing stare. ''You could have given her a mother's love.''

Kathi trembled and blinked back the moisture that burned at the back of her eyelids. A tear escaped. She brushed it away with the back of her hand.

She remembered the night so well. She'd been home, rocking her precious newborn, when the phone rang. She answered, and someone said, ''Hello, Kathi.'' Just two words, and yet they'd filled her with unspeakable dread. No matter that she'd taken a new name, moved to a new town, made no new friends to trip her up, someone had called her and known her real name.

And that night she knew that she had to give up her baby in order to keep her safe. She had to get Betsy to Ryder.

''But if you didn't want to be a mother to Betsy,

I'm glad you got her to me. A child needs family and love.''

"Let this go, Ryder. I love my daughter, and one day I'll be able to let her know that.''

Ryder stepped in front of her, so close his leg brushed against hers. "You could let her know it now. She needs her mother, and I'll never be the one to deny her knowing you. But, just for the record, you will never take her away from the Burning Pear. Not as long as I'm around to stop you.''

Kathi sucked in a shaky breath. "I didn't come here to take Betsy away from you, Ryder.''

"Then what did you come for?''

His question had any number of answers. To tell him the truth. To share the terror. To ease her own conscience. But it didn't really matter why she'd come. She'd have to leave without telling him anything. One hint of why she'd walked out on him, and Ryder would never let her leave again. She'd be in Kelman with Ryder and with Betsy. And so would the man who wanted her dead.

"I don't want you to go to trial for a murder you didn't commit. I suggest you talk to a couple of Shawn's friends in Fort Worth who would probably know if he had enemies.''

"Which friends would that be?''

"Julia Rodrigue, for one. She and Shawn lived together for almost a year. They split up about the time I was transferred to Fort Worth. When I met Shawn, he was still having a hard time with the breakup.''

"Did you ever meet her?''

"No.''

Ryder rubbed his fingers along the back of his neck. "Anyone else?"

"Bull Ruffkins. He and Shawn hung out together."

"I never heard him mention Bull."

"No, Shawn was always trying to impress you. He wouldn't bring up things that would make him look bad."

"Did either Julia or Bull work at Kincaid's?"

"No."

Ryder walked over to a small desk near the window. Rummaging through the clutter, he came up with a pencil and a pad of scratch paper. He printed a few letters and then stopped. "How do you spell Ruffkins?"

She told him and breathed a sigh of relief. Ryder believed this was the information she had traveled to Kelman to deliver. He would write down the names and let her walk away. And the killer could follow her out of town. Away from Ryder and away from Betsy.

There was even a chance that Julia or Bull could help him find the truth about who really murdered Shawn Priest. And if that ever happened, it would be safe for her to claim Betsy.

That is, if she was still alive to claim her.

"They're the only names I know, Ryder, and I really do need to be in San Antonio by morning." She swung her feet to the floor, determined to show Ryder that she could walk away on her own. The pain was sharp, overpowering. Wincing, she took a step and then stumbled.

Ryder caught her, his hands digging into the flesh

of her upper arms. He pulled her close. "Face it, Kathi. You're in no condition to travel tonight."

"I could. All I need is for you to help me to my car."

"The only place I'm helping you is to bed. I'll bring you the phone. You can call whoever's expecting you and tell him you can't make it." He swept her into his arms and headed down the hallway, not stopping until he reached the spare bedroom.

Thin shafts of moonlight streamed through the half-open blinds, glinting off the iron railings of the bed and painting silvery sprays of shadows over the worn quilt. Ryder crossed the room, pausing only to throw back the covers before he set her on the white sheets.

"I don't want to stay here alone with a man I don't even know." It was the only argument she could think of.

"You won't have to," he said, bending over and propping her feet on the bed. "You came here to help me. The least I can do is stay here and take care of you."

Kathi struggled for breath. Ryder. Here. The two of them in this bedroom. She shivered as the past cascaded down around her. The past and fear. And a longing so strong it robbed her of her last bit of fight.

"Okay, Ryder, you win. I'll stay one night."

Chapter Four

For a second Ryder stood too close. She could read desire in his eyes, and she had the crazy urge to pull him down to the bed beside her. But the second passed for both of them. He stepped back, putting a physical and an emotional distance between them.

"I need to clean up a little," she said, "and change out of these wet clothes."

"The bathroom's in there." He nodded toward a closed door on his left. "I can carry you or help you walk."

"Help me hobble," she said, already sliding to the floor. She held on to the bed until he got his arm around her. This time she maneuvered the few feet without putting any weight on her bad ankle.

Ryder opened the door with his free hand and guided her inside. She stopped in front of the mirror and stared into Horrorsville. She'd shed the wig earlier, and her own hair was damp and stuck to her head, except for a few strands that curled around her forehead. The heavy makeup she used as a disguise had apparently smeared when she'd swum in the shallow river, and her eyes were circled in smudged mascara. The powder and paint clung to her face in caked splotches that had mixed and dried with ample helpings of mud.

No wonder Arlo had looked at her as if she were some freak from a sideshow. "You're right," she said, twisting the faucet and adjusting the knobs until the water ran hot. "I have looked better."

"You'll do." He handed her a washcloth. His hand brushed hers when she took it from him. As always, the awareness level soared. Amazing, that after all she'd been through, he could still make her feel like a schoolgirl about to experience her first kiss.

He put a hand on the doorknob. "Can I get you anything else?"

"The toothbrush that's in my luggage, if you don't mind."

"Coming up." He turned and walked away, pulling the door closed behind him, knowing without her asking that she'd need a few minutes of privacy.

She'd have liked a bath or at least a shower, but the pain in her leg was beginning to ease a little, and she wasn't about to push her luck. So she did what she could with a washcloth, soap and a lot of hot water.

By the time Ryder returned with the toothbrush, she was ready for it and him. And her ankle had begun to throb. She brushed and rinsed without conviction, and he helped her back to bed.

"You have to get out of those clothes, Kathi. They're still damp and you don't want to get sick on top of everything else."

"I know." She pulled at the sticky T-shirt, peeling

it away from her body. "I have a nightshirt in my bag." A plain, cotton one with a red-wine stain in the center of the front. Definitely not her apparel of choice for sleeping over with a sexy cowboy. Not that she was actually going to sleep with him.

Funny, she had spent many lonely hours imagining what it would be like to see Ryder again. In none of the scenarios had she ever been a wet, dirty invalid or wearing shabby lingerie.

Ryder picked up her luggage and set it on the foot of the bed, but his gaze focused on her swollen ankle. Frowning, he leaned over and ran his fingers along the bottom edge of her jeans. "I don't see but one way you can get out of these. I'll have to cut you out."

She grimaced. "Then I guess I have no choice but to ruin a perfectly good pair of jeans."

"They won't be totally ruined. You can make them into cutoffs. I recall that you look terrific in shorts." Digging in his right front pocket, he pulled out an engraved pocketknife, one twice as large as the one she'd tried to use as a weapon earlier tonight. He pulled the blade from the metal niche and wiped his fingers across the sharp edges. "Are you ready?"

"As ready as I'll ever be, just take it easy with that blade."

He bent over and slipped the point of the knife below the hem of her damp jeans. His movements were steady and the knife was obviously razor-sharp. It sliced through the rough denim as easily as if it had been a ripe banana.

"You missed your calling," she said as he stepped

back to admire his handiwork. "You should have been a surgeon."

"I'll take that into consideration. If my knee doesn't hold up to bucking broncs, I may be looking for another profession sooner than I'd intended."

His knee. The image came to her again, the car plowing into him and sending him flying through the air. She wasn't the only one who'd paid for her mistake one black morning. But he wasn't even limping now.

"Anything else I can get you?" he asked.

"No, you've done more than enough already. I guess I haven't shown it, but I do appreciate your help."

"I couldn't turn down a beautiful woman in distress. They'd make me turn in my Stetson," he teased.

"And where would you be without that?"

"Naked," he admitted. "And a lost soul." He smiled. "Now you need to get some sleep. Are you sure you can manage those jeans by yourself?"

"I think so." With a flick of her wrist, she tugged her shirt out of her waistband and unsnapped her jeans. Holding her stomach in, she pulled down on the zipper. It caught on the wet fabric and refused to budge.

Without a word, Ryder leaned over her and fitted his large fingers around the minute metal pull. He yanked hard, and the zipper responded, gaping open. When she looked up, he was staring at the sliver of bare flesh that stretched from her waist to just below her navel.

It was only his eyes that probed the erogenous

zone, but her insides couldn't have burned any hotter if it had been his fingertips or even his lips.

She tried to say something, but her mind seemed to have deserted her and her throat closed so tightly she could barely catch her breath. Finally she managed a murmur that seemed to come from someone else. "I think I can handle the rest on my own."

"If that's the way you want it." He turned and walked to the door.

She ached to call to him as the door slammed shut, longed to tell him that this *wasn't* the way she wanted it. It had never been. She wanted his hands on her naked body, wanted his breath to mingle with hers. But she couldn't have him for a night and then just walk out of his life again. The shattered remains of her heart could never take it.

Throwing her arms over her head, she wiggled out of the cotton T-shirt and let it drop to the quilt. She *could* undress herself—undress herself and sleep alone. She'd done both of them for the past two years. It was a lonely existence, but it kept her alive.

And no matter that Ryder didn't understand or appreciate her walking out on him. It had kept him alive, too.

RYDER SAT in the overstuffed chair thinking and watching Kathi. He'd come in to check on her when he couldn't sleep, and he'd stayed the biggest part of the night. Asleep, her face scrubbed clean of the excess makeup, she looked years younger than her twenty-four years. Nor did she seem old enough to be a mother, but the likeness to the daughter he adored was evident in the nose that turned up ever so slightly, the thick lashes, the heart-shaped face.

Earlier tonight, when he'd helped her undress, the old fire had flared so hot it had almost melted his ability to reason. Even now, he was so affected by her nearness that it was all he could do not to climb into the bed with her and hold her in his arms while she slept.

But the facts hadn't changed. Kathi didn't want him or their daughter. It had been almost a year since Betsy had been delivered by a stranger to the doorstep at the Burning Pear. They had been celebrating his mother's sixtieth birthday. The whole family had been there.

At the time, he and his brothers had been sure that the baby was not theirs. All four of them had declared unequivocally that they had not fathered a child. They were certain that the claim that she was a Randolph had been invented as a way to bilk money from the family.

Only his mother had felt differently. From the moment she first held her granddaughter, she'd been sure that Betsy was a Randolph.

For a long time Ryder had held on to the belief that Betsy wasn't his child. Not that he had forgotten for a minute the nights he and Kathi had made love until the sun came up. But they had been careful. They'd used protection, *almost* all of the time. But the main reason he'd believed Betsy couldn't be his child was because he'd been so certain Kathi Sable would never desert her own flesh and blood.

It had taken a DNA test to convince him, but finally he had realized that he had never really known Kathi Sable.

He rubbed a spot over his right temple, new questions pushing their way to the forefront of his mind. If Kathi had no feelings for him, why was she so concerned that he'd been questioned in Shawn's murder? Why would she have traveled to Kelman to see if she could help?

He stretched his weary muscles, the need for sleep numbing his brain. Nothing that had happened tonight seemed to make sense, but at least Kathi knew him well enough to realize he hadn't killed Shawn. Apparently she was satisfied to have him and his family continue to raise Betsy.

He stood slowly, walked to the window and stared into the moonlit pastures that surrounded Arlo's house. Kathi stirred, moaning softly. Part of him ached to go to her, to take her in his arms and soothe her mind and body. But the rest of him, the sane part, knew that it would be a bad mistake, and he'd already made too many of them where she was concerned.

She planned to walk out of his life again as soon as she could get around on her bad ankle. He planned to let her.

He raked his fingers through his already mussed hair. Tomorrow he'd talk to Branson and decide how to handle locating and questioning Julia Rodrigue and Bull Ruffkins. If they knew anything at all about what had led to Shawn's murder, they might be able to clear him as a suspect.

He padded back to the chair, falling into it and propping his feet on the bed rail. For a second, the face of Shawn Priest floated in front of him, his mouth open as if he wanted to tell Ryder something. A minute later, Ryder's eyes gave in to the weight of his lids and he couldn't seem to think at all.

It was nearly dawn when he opened his eyes and ambled back to the small room at the end of the hall.

RYDER WOKE to a pounding in his head. His eyes jerked open, but it took a second or two for them to focus. And a second more for him to realize that the pounding was at the door. He kicked off the Mexican blanket that was tangled around his legs and hopped across the room while he pulled on his jeans. He had to catch himself on the back edge of a chair to keep from falling.

"I'm coming, Arlo." His voice was heavy with the dregs of sleep. He swung the door open. Arlo stood there, fully dressed, though the sun had barely broken over the horizon.

"I hate to bother you, Ryder, but you have a call from Branson. He's looking for you and he says it's urgent."

"I called the house last night and left a message that I was staying over."

"He knows where you are. I don't think that's the problem."

Ryder swallowed an irritated curse. If Branson was tracking him down at sunup, it wasn't to deliver good news. More than likely it had something to do with Shawn's murder. But surely there wasn't a warrant out for his arrest.

They couldn't possibly have enough evidence against him. He was innocent.

"You can take the call in the kitchen," Arlo said.

Ryder hurried into the kitchen and grabbed the receiver. "Ryder here. What's up, Branson?"

"Another body on Randolph property. This one was fresh, killed a few hours ago."

Ryder swallowed a curse. "Who now?"

"No identification as yet, but it was a man, looked to be in his early forties, died from three gunshot wounds to the chest."

"Three?"

"Evidently the killer wasn't taking any chances that the victim might survive."

"Where was the body found?"

"On the old Larker place, the land we bought from him last June."

"Down by the old campgrounds?"

"How did you know that?"

"I'll fill you in later. Anything else?"

"Yeah. We found a car there, too. It's registered to a woman named Susan Campbell from Mobile, Alabama."

Susan Campbell. So that was what the black-haired version of Kathi Sable called herself. The plot thickened by the minute.

"Do you have any leads in the murder?"

"No. I'm out at the scene of the crime now, but I haven't turned up anything concrete except the body and the car. There are a couple of other sets of fresh tire tracks, though. Another car and a pickup truck, at least that's what it looks like to me. I'm going to have casts made of the prints, but even that may not get us anywhere."

"I can save you a little trouble. At least one set

of the tracks belong to me.'' Ryder dropped the bombshell and then waited for Branson to react.

''I hope you have a damn good explanation for this, Ryder. If not, you just dug that hole you're in a couple of miles deeper.''

''Then we better get out the best bulldozer we have.'' Ryder's mind revved into overtime. ''I'm on my way out there, Branson. We'll talk then.''

Ryder hung up before Branson had a chance to ask more questions. He didn't have any answers, but all of a sudden, he was certain that the woman sleeping down the hall did. And it was past time she started spilling the real truth.

KATHI HELD ON to the tile wall of the shower and stood under the hot spray. Her ankle still throbbed like crazy, but at least she'd managed to walk to the bathroom with only the aid of the walls for support. She had to bring her body back to life and convince Ryder she was healthy enough to make it out of town on her own. She lifted her leg and winced in pain.

Stepping out of the shower, she grabbed a towel, gave her body a brisk once-over and then plopped onto the toilet seat while she pulled on clean underwear. Fortunately she'd also packed a pair of shorts. They'd fit over her leg without having to slash out a seam.

When she got back to the room, Ryder was waiting for her. ''You must be feeling better.''

''Actually, I feel great,'' she lied. ''The ankle barely hurts now.''

''Good. Then you won't have any trouble going to the sheriff's office with me later.''

"I've told you everything I know, Ryder. I'm not talking to the sheriff. There's no reason for me to."

"I think we should let my brother Branson be the judge of that. Not only is he the sheriff, but it just so happens he's spent his morning at the same spot where I found you hiding last night from a would-be attacker."

"What was he doing out there?"

"Picking up a body. Apparently you weren't the only one being chased last night. The other person wasn't nearly as lucky. He took three bullets in the chest."

She listened as Ryder repeated what he'd heard from his brother. His face was strained, his eyes glazed with a hardness she'd never seen on him before. Her own stomach rolled sickeningly, but she forced her mind to stay sharp. "I had nothing to do with the murder, Ryder. It's not connected to my visit."

"I find that a little hard to believe."

She sank down on the edge of the bed, her legs too shaky to hold her up. It was starting all over again. The killing. The fear. "You should have let me leave last night when I wanted to."

"And then you could have conveniently been miles away from here when the body was found."

"I told you last night, Ryder. I was simply in the wrong place at the wrong time. The attacker was probably desperate. He could have been looking for someone to run off the road and rob. When it didn't work with me, he may have just found another victim."

"The Brothers Grimm wrote more believable stories than that.'' He set the mug of strong coffee he'd poured for her on the bedside table. ''I'm going out to meet Branson at the scene of the crime. When we leave there, I'll circle back here and pick you up. You and I are going to take a ride to Branson's office, and this time I expect the truth.''

''I told you the truth. I have no idea who was murdered last night.''

''Maybe not, but you know who you were hiding from.'' He reached over and picked up her wig, burying his fingers in the thick black hair. ''And you know who you planned to fool with this.'' He dropped the wig back to the table and then brushed his hands together as if the fake hair had somehow contaminated them.

He didn't wait for an answer. Instead, he turned and strode out of the room.

Her heart constricted. He was angry now. She'd been that way at first. But it hadn't taken a long time for the anger to evolve into fear and then desperation. She had to get out of here. Quick. Before Ryder was snagged by the same web that entangled her.

That is, if he wasn't already.

THE WIND was persistent, blowing dust, whipping Ryder's hair back from his face, cutting through his light jacket. He was thankful for it. The sensation was like a slap in the face, and he needed the cold to keep his mind on what was being said around him. Needed it to keep from drifting back to last night's events in this same place.

The one fact he kept coming back to was that he'd been the one who suggested this spot for his talk with

Kathi. Still, she was the one who wanted to meet somewhere private. Had she called someone when she left the Roadhouse and set up a meeting between—

Now he was thinking crazy. Kathi hadn't helped set up a murder. Besides, she'd been scared half to death when he'd found her.

Branson left his deputy, Gordon, taking pictures of Kathi's car. He walked over to Ryder, his face a study of concentration. Like the rest of Ryder's brothers, he liked life best when it was riding a smooth road, but he could handle whatever came his way.

Today he was all lawman. A man had been murdered, and in Kelman, that was still a rare and shocking occurrence. He pulled his western hat down low to shade his eyes from the morning sun. "It was an ugly sight. Be glad you missed it."

"I take it that means the body has already gone to the morgue."

"Yeah. I didn't see any reason to let it sit any longer in the sun. I have a roll of pictures showing the exact spot where we found it and the position it was in."

"How *did* you find it?" Ryder asked.

"I got a call at four this morning. It was Zeke Wilson's son Gerald. Evidently he and his girlfriend had come out here to neck. They stumbled over the body."

"Necking at four in the morning? That's a little late for a high-school boy to be out, isn't it?"

"That was my first question. But Gerald said he and Maria Garcia actually found the body around eleven. Maria was supposed to be at her girlfriend's house, and he was afraid that telling me about the body would get her in trouble. Finally, after he'd stayed awake half the night worrying, he woke up his dad and told him about the body. His dad insisted he call me.''

"I guess we're just lucky Gerald and Maria didn't happen out here while the killer was doing his dirty work.''

"Yeah.'' Branson bit his bottom lip. "Lucky you weren't out here then, too. Are you ready to tell me what that's all about? And while you're at it, tell me why your name and phone number was written on a piece of paper that we found in the front seat of Susan Campbell's car.''

"So that's why you called me this morning.''

"My first concern was that you were all right. Since you are, I need answers.''

Ryder buried his hands in his pockets. "You're not thinking I had anything to do with the murder, are you?''

Branson laid a hand on Ryder's shoulder. "That was the one possibility that never crossed my mind. But we need to talk, fast, before the media gets hold of this.''

"And before the good ranger who's investigating Shawn's murder comes over to escort me to jail.''

"So, exactly who is Susan Campbell and why were you out here last night?''

Ryder took a deep breath. "First, the woman's name is not Susan Campbell. Apparently that's an alias she uses. Her real name is Kathi Sable.''

Branson's jaw dropped open. He shook his head

slowly and then nailed Ryder with a piercing stare. "Not *your* Kathi Sable? Not Betsy's mother?"

"One and the same."

The morning sun bore down on them as Ryder told Branson the whole story, beginning with the moment Kathi had walked through the door at the Roadhouse. Even as he described the events of the night before, he recognized the surreal quality of what he was saying. From the moment he'd known for certain that Betsy was his daughter, he'd told all of his brothers the truth about his relationship with Betsy's mother. At least the truth as he knew it then. The reality of it had changed dramatically over the past few hours.

Branson asked few questions as Ryder talked, but Ryder could almost see the wheels turning in his mind.

"I know you used to be in love with this woman, Ryder, but don't be blind to her true character."

He used to be in love with her. That was an accurate description, but it didn't touch on the feelings he'd had last night. Love, attraction, lust...who knew what made his heart and body react so strongly to the sight of her?

Branson leaned on Ryder's front fender. "What do you really know about Kathi Sable?"

Ryder looked Branson in the eye. "I know she's Betsy's mother. That counts for something, Branson."

"I'm not sure it counts with her. This has all the makings of a frame-up."

"I don't see it that way. I told you Kathi was afraid last night. I don't think she faked that."

"Maybe she was afraid because something went

wrong. You were supposed to follow in five minutes. You said yourself, you were delayed by a flat tire on your truck. Was the tire vandalized or did it go flat on its own?''

Damn. He hadn't even thought of that. Maybe someone had known he was supposed to follow Kathi to a deserted spot. They may have wanted to make sure he didn't show up on time. That would explain the slash in his tire better than anything he'd come up with.

"This is all just speculation, Branson. We don't have proof of anything, except the fact that someone was murdered out here last night and that Kathi and I were also out here.''

"I know." He ran his hand over the butt of his gun. "You're already wanted for the murder of Shawn Priest, Ryder. Now you just happen to show up at the scene of another murder, a few minutes to an hour before it happens. I *have* to speculate. The detective who's building a case against you certainly will.''

Ryder stared at the creek and the spot where he'd found Kathi hiding last night. "I can't accuse Kathi of anything until I know the truth, Branson. She's Betsy's mother.''

Branson dug the toe of his right boot into the hard, dry earth. "I know how you feel about Betsy, Ryder. We all love her. She's as much a part of the family as you or me, and I'm not out to pin anything on her mother. I just can't close my eyes to the obvious.''

"Is that what you think I'm doing?''

"I think you're more trusting than I am.''

"*Everyone's* more trusting than you are.''

"I want to talk to her, Ryder. Do you want to bring her into my office or do you want me to go with you to Arlo's?"

"I'll bring her in. I've already told her you'd want to question her." Ryder opened the door of his truck. "Question her, but go easy, will you?"

"I'll go as easy as she'll let me. If she gives me the whole truth and not some cock-and-bull story about how she popped out of the woodwork because she wanted to tell you a couple of names."

Ryder walked away, knowing Branson was right but still hating to turn him loose on Kathi. Branson was a good man, gentle at times, especially with Betsy. And no one could ask for a more dependable brother, but he had always been the suspicious one of the family.

According to one of his mom's favorite stories, Branson even questioned a mall Santa Claus when he was only three. He demanded to know if he really had a list of who was naughty and who was nice because Branson didn't think he could spell everybody's name.

Ryder climbed into his truck and revved the engine, anxious to get back to Arlo's and talk to Kathi one more time himself. If she did know something, it would be a lot better for her if she talked willingly, before Branson dragged the truth out of her.

ARLO POURED the bucket of slop into the trough. He was a cattleman, but he liked his pork, and it was no trouble to raise a few pigs along with his cows.

His heart wasn't in his work this morning, though. Neither was his mind. It was back in the house with

Kathi Sable. The woman was a looker—at least she was this morning since she'd washed away the mud and two tons of runny makeup—but she was a poor liar.

Ryder saw what he wanted to in her. Arlo could understand that. A man never wanted to think a woman he'd made love to was less than wonderful, especially if that woman had given birth to his child. But this woman had duplicity coming out of her pores.

She had something to do with the murder down by the creek last night and now she was running scared. He'd seen it in her eyes when she'd sat across the kitchen table from him a few minutes ago. She'd been friendly enough at first but the second he'd mentioned the murder, she'd clammed up, her mood chilling so fast he could have gotten frostbite.

He turned and looked back to the house. He'd tell Ryder what he thought, but that was as far as he'd go. He wasn't a lawman anymore.

A slamming noise grabbed his attention. Metal on metal. He pushed his hat back and walked around the barn, trying to find the source of the racket. An engine started, its coughing sputter fading to a hum. His truck.

He turned just as a cloud of dust sprang up on the road leading to and from his house. A string of curses rolled loudly from his tongue. Kathi Sable was driving away, hell-bent for leather, and she was leaving in his truck.

Chapter Five

Mary Randolph slid the pan of biscuits from the oven. The tops were golden, just the way they should be, and the biscuits had puffed up all round and flaky. The sight and the smell of them soothed her a little. Still, she was worried sick about her youngest son.

Poor Ryder. He had always been the most impulsive of her boys. Had always jumped into life as if it would leave him behind if he hesitated for a second. But for all his impetuousness, he would never so much as hurt someone's feelings if there was any way around it.

Now he was being questioned in a murder case, and if that weren't bad enough, another man's body had been found on Randolph property. Her phone had been ringing steadily ever since the news broke. She appreciated the concern of their friends and neighbors, but talking about the problem had made it that much harder for her.

Thankfully, Branson's wife, Lacy, was such a dear. She'd taken Betsy off for the afternoon so that Mary could have some time to rest. Only she couldn't rest. She wiped her hands on her apron and walked back to the counter and her salad fixings. She had to keep busy, or else the worry would pull her under.

The youngest child always had a special place in a mother's heart. She smiled in spite of herself. *All* her boys had a special place. It was just that the one who was in trouble at the moment was the one who tugged hardest at her heartstrings.

It had been that way since they were children, like the time Ryder had fallen from his horse while participating in the barrel-riding competition. He'd spent the night in the hospital with a mild concussion, and she'd stayed awake all night watching over him. Watching and praying.

Only Ryder wasn't a boy anymore. He was a man, with man-sized problems and she no longer had all the answers. She sighed. It was times like these that she missed her boys' father the most.

Last night, she'd lain awake for hours, all alone in her big bed, longing for the husband who'd died so many years ago. Most of the time she did all right with just the wonderful memories and the joy that had come with raising their four sons. But times like these, when anxiety spilled all through her life, she missed him so desperately, she could hardly stand it.

Times like these. Hard times, when the days should be overflowing with happiness. Next week, Betsy would have her first birthday party. They were guessing at the date, but she was sure they weren't far from the right one. Birthdays were always a major affair at Burning Pear, but she didn't see how this could be much of a celebration with Betsy's daddy worrying about defending himself in a murder case.

"So here you are."

The voice startled Mary. She caught her breath as Lacy waltzed into the room, balancing Betsy on her right hip.

"I should have known you'd be in the kitchen slaving away." Lacy switched Betsy to the other hip. "I don't know what you're cooking, but it smells wonderful."

"It's just pork chops and some peas and corn. And I threw together some biscuits. Ryder always likes hot biscuits with pork chops."

"*Just* pork chops." Lacy swung Betsy in a half circle, and then deposited her in her high chair. "Why don't you let me finish that salad, and you sit down and keep your granddaughter company."

"Ba-ba ca-da." Betsy contributed to the conversation and then drummed on the tray in front of her.

"See, Betsy agrees with me," Lacy said. "She knows she's already worn me out. She's ready for fresh meat. Besides, you're not supposed to overdo it."

"You've been listening to those sons of mine. They think I'm getting old, but I can work circles around them any day of the week." But still, Mary took Lacy up on her offer. She was a little tired, and Lacy was such a dear to think about that. "What did the two of you do all afternoon?" she asked, pulling up a kitchen chair and sitting down next to her granddaughter's high chair.

"We took a ride in Betsy's little red wagon and then I pushed her in the airplane swing her uncle Langley made for her. She's already a little daredevil. The higher the swing went, the more she laughed.''

Betsy reached over and poked her fingers in Mary's graying topknot. "Oh no you don't, young lady. You pull too hard." She took the tiny fingers in her hand and kissed them.

"How much salad should I make?" Lacy asked.

"Use all the lettuce. I don't know what's up, but Langley and Dillon both called and said they'd be over tonight to talk to Branson, so, I called Danielle and Ashley and invited them to join us for dinner, as well. No use for them to have to cook if their husbands are over here."

"Just trying to save them a little work, huh. And it has nothing to do with having both your grandchildren at your dinner table."

Mary chuckled. "You know me too well."

Mary played with Betsy, walking her favorite toy cow across her high-chair tray while making mooing sounds. Betsy mimicked her. She was so adorable, and yet tonight even Betsy couldn't take her mind off the problems that were plaguing Ryder.

"Did Branson say what this meeting is about?" she asked.

"No, but I'm sure it has to do with the body that was found out at the old Larker place. The last I heard, the body hasn't been identified."

"I wish that old campgrounds *still* belonged to the Larkers. I don't like the idea of another body showing up on Randolph land. I don't like it a bit. It'll be just like that Texas Ranger who's been questioning Ryder to try and blame this killing on him, too."

Lacy turned and offered her a reassuring smile.

"Branson is working hard to find evidence that will clear Ryder."

"It's just too bad he turned the investigation over to the rangers. If Branson was handling the case, we wouldn't have all these shenanigans, with people running around accusing innocent men."

Lacy held the carrots under the faucet, washing them thoroughly. "Branson didn't have a choice. If he hadn't asked them to step in, they would have taken the case anyway. The body was found on Burning Pear, and with the sheriff's brother under suspicion, they had to get involved."

"Then the rangers better get out there and find the real killer and leave my boy alone. I can't imagine how anyone could believe he would shoot his friend."

"I'm sure the questioning was just a formality. Everyone knows Ryder is innocent."

Mary brushed her fingers through Betsy's hair, pushing a wayward curl back from her eyebrows. "I just don't like all this questioning and speculation. I mean it's got to be taking its toll on Ryder. He didn't even come home last night. Instead, he stayed over at Arlo's. I'm sure they spent the evening discussing the murder investigation."

Lacy stopped chopping and walked over to stand beside Mary. "Ryder's going to do the right thing, and he's not going to jail."

"I hope you're right," Mary said. "And I hope this is all cleared up soon. Poor Betsy doesn't have a mother around, and now her daddy has to spend all his time just trying to prove his innocence. That's not the way the courts in this country were designed to work.''

''Branson doesn't expect this case to go to court. He thinks the rangers are just trying to cover all the bases.''

''That's what I'm counting on.'' Mary ran her fingers up her neck, collecting hairs that had strayed from her topknot. ''I've been thinking a lot about Betsy's mother lately. I just don't understand how a woman could walk away from her own flesh and blood.''

Lacy shot her a strange look, as if she'd just admitted to being a Martian. ''How did Betsy's mother get into this conversation?''

''I guess it's the upcoming birthday. A mother should never miss her child's first birthday, unless she can't possibly make it home.''

The conversation paused, interrupted by the sound of a truck pulling into the back driveway. Lacy stepped to the screen door and peered out. ''The odor of those biscuits must stretch a long way.''

''Is that Branson?''

''Yes, and Ryder's with him.''

Mary took a deep breath and tried not to show her anxiety. It would only upset Ryder, and he had enough to worry about without adding her to his list. Besides, all of her sons would be here tonight, and if the Randolph men set their mind to something, pity the opponent that stepped in their way.

Ryder walked through the back door, and despite Mary's determination, her heart fell at the sight of him. There was no sign of his trademark smile. No hint of teasing in his eyes.

Betsy didn't notice. She threw up her arms. "Da, da, da, da."

Ryder lifted her from her high chair and hugged her tight. Then he tossed her in the air, like always, and she broke into her sweet, gurgling laugh.

Ryder's dad had played with him the same way when Ryder was Betsy's age. Tossing Ryder in the air and then catching him and settling him on his broad shoulders for a ride out to the corral to see the horses. Ryder had always loved horses.

She swallowed hard and wished he were her little boy again and that a kiss could cure all his hurts. But those days were gone forever.

RYDER SAT in the small stucco building that served as the ranch headquarters and tried to imagine why Kathi had stolen Arlo's truck and skipped out. He was sure there was a reason other than the one his brother Branson kept ascribing to her actions.

"It sounds awful foul to me," Langley said, "and I'm usually the optimistic one."

Ryder spread his hands out on the table. "I know how it sounds," Ryder insisted, "but I was there, and there's more to it than that." He paced the large rectangular room. He and his brothers had driven out right after dinner for a family conference. All for one and one for all; that was the Randolph way. But he was the one whose freedom was at stake.

"Let's just look at the facts," Dillon said in his best senatorial voice. "Kathi Sable shows up after all this time and wants to meet you in an isolated setting. You follow her there, and find her hiding from a would-be attacker. The next morning, a man's body is found in the very same area."

Ryder stopped pacing. "But remember that I was the one who suggested the spot."

"Was the campground your first choice?" Langley asked.

"No, my first choice was the Burning Pear. She refused to come here."

Branson stroked his chin. "Which makes sense if she was setting you up. The Burning Pear would be the last place she'd agree to."

Langley leaned forward, resting his elbows on the round wooden table. "The man you saw leaving the area when you arrived there last night might be working with Kathi. He might have murdered the victim before you even got there."

Ryder listened to his brothers. He knew they made sense, but then they hadn't seen what he had. "Kathi was scared half to death when I found her."

"Or at least she seemed that way," Dillon said.

Ryder released an exasperated breath. "It would have been hard to fake the look of terror in her eyes and the lack of color in her face. Besides, she jumped in the creek. No one would jump in that murky water at night without a very good reason."

"I think she had a reason," Branson said. "And I'm sure she considers it a good one."

Dillon looked skeptical. "Let's just explore possibilities. Suppose Kathi and a friend wanted someone dead. You are already a suspect for murder, so if she can lure you to the scene of the crime, you will be the first person under suspicion for this new killing."

Ryder tried to see Kathi in the role Dillon had assigned her. The scenario didn't ring true, or maybe he just didn't want it to. "I know you all want to help, and I appreciate the thought and the effort, but the way I see it, we can't know anything until we find Kathi."

"I agree." Branson stood and braced himself against the back of his chair. "I have an all-points bulletin out on her now."

"Has she been spotted at all?" Langley asked.

"A gas-station employee reported seeing a woman who fit her description in Batesville around noon, and a man who owns a truck stop near Loma Alta reported that she stopped there a couple of hours ago. In both cases, it was primarily the limp they remembered, but they sounded pretty reliable."

"She hasn't put a lot of distance between her and Kelman," Dillon said. "It sounds like she's zigzagging her way west."

"Probably thinks she's covering her tracks," Branson said. "She's sticking to back roads and possibly having to stop to put her leg up if it's giving her a lot of trouble. We should have her in custody by morning."

"Fine." Ryder rammed his hands deep into his pockets. As much as he appreciated his brothers' help and valued their advice, he had to go with his gut feeling on this one. "I don't want Kathi arrested," he said, his gaze locked with Branson's. "I just want to talk to her."

"I have a murder to investigate, Ryder, at least for now. I'm not sure how long it will be until I'm told to give it over to a 'less personally involved' law officer. But in the meantime, Kathi Sable is not only a suspect in the murder, but she stole Arlo's truck and ran rather than come into my office for questioning. That's not a sign of innocence.''

Ryder felt the exasperation building inside him. His muscles tightened; his tone took on a sharpness he seldom used around the ranch. "Kathi is Betsy's mother, Branson. You can't just treat her like some common criminal.''

"I'm a sheriff, Ryder. I don't have the luxury of trust.''

"You didn't have the luxury of trust even when you weren't a sheriff. Dillon should remember that. You doubted his wife was telling the truth when her life was in danger.''

"I was wrong about Ashley. And for the record, I hope I'm just as wrong about Kathi Sable.'' Branson stared at Ryder. "Betsy may be your daughter, but you're not the only one who loves that little girl.''

Dillon pushed his chair back from the table and stood. "Okay, guys, let's not let this get out of hand. We're all on the same side here. We want to apprehend the guilty and prove Ryder's innocence, but I agree with Ryder. We can't just forget that Kathi Sable is Betsy's mother.''

Branson exhaled sharply. "What's that supposed to mean?''

"It just means that while I'm willing to consider all possibilities, I'm not comfortable jumping to the conclusion that Betsy's mother is out to send Ryder to jail on a murder rap. If she doesn't want to take care of Betsy, then it seems like she'd want Ryder around.''

"Most mothers would," Branson agreed. "But none of us are so naive that we think *all* mothers are noble and loving or that mothers always put their children first. We don't know enough about this woman to make assumptions as to what she's capable or not capable of doing."

"I told you what I know," Ryder said.

"You did, and now we're all tired and reduced to running in circles and getting nowhere," Dillon said. "I think it's time we call it a night."

No one disagreed with him, least of all Ryder. He had business to take care of.

Langley walked over and laid a hand on Ryder's shoulder. "You know we're behind you, little brother."

"Right," Dillon agreed. "If you need anything, you can call, day or night. Family first. It's always been that way and always will be."

Langley nodded. "And things could be a lot worse. Imagine if Kathi had grabbed Betsy and taken her along with Arlo's truck."

Branson reached for his Stetson. "In that case I'd hate to be in her shoes."

"But she could want custody when this is over," Dillon reminded them.

Branson walked to the door and then turned. "Then I guess she'd have to fight all of us."

"Damn straight," Langley agreed.

They said their goodbyes and Ryder climbed into his pickup. Betsy would be sleeping by now, safe and sound with her grandmother keeping close watch. But where was Betsy's mother, and who was keeping watch over her?

He passed the ranch house and drove out to the road. It would be hard to find a woman and a truck that had eluded the police all day, but he had nothing better to do than join the search.

Nothing but sleep, and he'd done without that many a night and for much less reason.

KATHI HOBBLED from the lumpy bed to the hotel dresser. Leaning against it, she peered into the cloudy mirror. Sweat beaded on her forehead, an outward sign of the fear that rode her shaky nerves and the acid that pooled in her stomach. She should have forced down the ham sandwich at the truck stop, but by then her stomach had already been too upset to face more than the cold cola she had used to wash down the handful of aspirin.

A sudden bout of chills shook her. She stumbled across the room and fell on the bed. A cheap motel in a back-roads Texas town. Surely she was safe enough here that she could risk grabbing a few hours' sleep. Bending from the waist, she slipped a pillow under her ankle.

If she'd been able to keep it elevated today, it would probably be well on the way to recovery by now. Instead, she'd pushed it and herself to the limit, sitting upright behind the wheel of a truck for hours and hours. When the pain became so excruciating that she had to stop, she'd hidden the truck away in thickets of brush off isolated roads.

Now exhaustion stole into her mind, a veil that made thinking impossible. She closed her eyes and drifted away. And then the dreams came—this time good ones. She held her baby girl close. "Mommy loves you, Betsy. Mommy loves you so very much."

THE SUN SHONE through the front window of Ryder's pickup. He squinted in the glare. He'd driven most of the night, not pulling over for a rest stop until his eyes had refused to stay open and it had been dangerous to keep going.

At first he'd been determined to be the man to find Kathi and take her back to Kelman. Now, he'd welcome a vibration from the pager at his waist, a message from Branson that Kathi had been picked up by a trooper.

Strange, he'd spent the past twenty-one months of his life resenting Kathi—first for walking out on him when he was injured and later for deserting their child.

But all his rationalizing had not changed the way he felt about her. He'd known that the minute he'd found her cowering under the brush, scared half to death and still fighting.

But she hadn't been honest with him. It was clear she was running from someone. But who and why? And why had she picked this moment to walk back into his life, unless the trouble she was in had something to do with Shawn's murder?

The questions had haunted his mind all night, but he was no closer to coming up with answers. His stomach growled and he took an exit that promised food. Whatever he found, it wouldn't be as good as what his mom would cook up at home this morning. But as long as the coffee was strong and hot, he wouldn't complain.

THE TRUCK STOP bustled with activity. Evidently the kings of the road started their day at dawn. Ryder made his way to a booth in the back. A few seconds later, a young waitress with a coffeepot in hand flashed him a smile and stuck a stained menu in his face.

"Coffee?"

"Strong and black."

"You got it, cowboy."

She leaned over and poured a long stream of brew into a white mug. She lingered, and he felt the gaze as he studied the breakfast offerings.

"You're Ryder Randolph, aren't you?"

He looked up. "Do I know you?"

"Not yet, but you could if you wanted to." She flashed a wide smile and flipped the ends of her hair in a move she probably considered seductive. "I used to see you on television all the time, you know, on that cable station that shows rodeos late at night. You are the same man, aren't you?"

"I'm Ryder Randolph, and I ride broncs, at least I used to."

"I knew it."

She put the coffeepot down on his table and propped her hands on her hips, apparently oblivious to the fact that other customers were waiting or that she hadn't taken his order.

"Lucille—she's another waitress here—anyway, we used to work the night shift together and we'd watch the rodeo and bet on who we thought would pick up the most points." She leaned closer, exposing a fair amount of cleavage. "I always picked you.

Not because you were good, but because you were s-o-o-o-o sexy. And here you are in person.''

"In person and hungry."

"I'm sorry." She blushed. "I'm going on and on, but would you mind giving me your autograph? Lucille will never believe I saw you if you don't."

"I will, and I'll write something extra-special if you'll get my order up double-quick. Two eggs over easy, a side of sausage and toast."

"You got it." She handed him a charge ticket, turning it over so that he had the full back of it to write on. "Sign it to Marsha."

"Okay." He started writing and then stopped. "Tell me, Marsha, where would someone go around here if they were looking for a place to catch a few hours' sleep."

"There's a Holiday Inn Express on the highway, next exit. I don't know what it costs, but it's nice."

"No, I'm looking for something more out-of-the-way, a local place, rather than a chain."

She eyed him suspiciously. "You're the second person who's asked that in the past few hours."

"Really. Who else asked?"

"A woman. She came hobbling in here about two this morning. Poor thing. Her ankle was so swollen she could barely walk. She ordered a ham sandwich on wheat, but she barely touched it. She just drank her cola, went to the bathroom and left."

"Did you give her the name of a motel?"

"The SunUp Inn. I wouldn't stay there, but some folks do."

"Where would I find this place?"

Her eyes lit up as if she'd just answered the million-dollar question. "You're looking for her, aren't you?"

"Right." He pulled out his billfold and took out a twenty. He dropped it onto the table by his cup. "So how do I find the SunUp?"

He scribbled down the directions as she talked. Then he stood and plopped his hat back on his head.

"What about breakfast?"

"Cancel the order." He started out the door.

She ran behind him. "What about my autograph?" she said, pushing her blank ticket toward him.

He took the pen and paper from her hand and started writing, scribbling his usual line: "Winners jump on fast and hang on tight." Then he added one more, just for Marsha: "You just made my day. Ryder Randolph."

He rushed out the door without looking back, but her voice followed him. "Lucille is going to just die of envy."

RYDER PULLED into the parking lot of SunUp Inn. The building was one-story, the rooms laid out in a long, straight line of doors and narrow windows. The place had probably been nice a few decades ago, but it had fallen into serious disrepair. Still, there were a couple of cars in the lot and one ancient pickup truck.

Arlo's truck was nowhere to be seen. Disappointment settled in Ryder's stomach like week-old cornbread. He brought his own truck to a crawl and pulled to the back of the building.

Bingo! There was Arlo's truck, parked off the pavement and out of sight of the road. A fat cat who'd probably dined on too many rats strolled

across the hood as if it was his private property. But
if the cat had been rolling in fresh tuna he wouldn't
have felt any better than Ryder did at the moment.

He drove back to the front of the motel, parked
and strode into the door marked Office. The sign at
the desk said Ring for Service. Ryder didn't bother.
The registration book was on the counter. Apparently
computers had not yet arrived at the SunUp Inn. A
minute later Ryder was knocking on Kathi Sable's
door.

KATHI TOSSED in the bed, torn between a banging
that ripped through her temples and the dregs of deep
sleep. The banging won. Her heart jumped to her
throat as she realized that the noise was coming from
the front door.

She unwound from the covers and threw her feet
to the carpet, adrenaline finally kicking in. She'd
dodged a killer for almost two years, always on the
move, always in disguise. Always in fear. What a
sad quirk of fate, if her time finally ran out in this
dilapidated motel in a town she couldn't name.

She scanned the room. There was one door and
one window, both facing the front of the building.
Escape was impossible. That left ''stand and fight''
as the only reasonable choice. A ceramic lamp base
or a sliver of glass from a broken mirror would be
her choice of weapons.

Heart pounding, she stretched and peered out the
peek hole. Ryder. Terror rushed from her body, replaced by another kind of dread that defied reason.
She'd looked him in the eye and lied to him once in

the past twenty-four hours. God help her, but she wasn't sure she was strong enough to do it again.

He raised his fist, ready to hammer it against the door. Before he could, she turned the dead bolt and swung it open. "Do you always make house calls this time of the morning?" she asked as he stepped past her.

"Not always. Only when someone I helped out steals my friend's truck."

"I didn't steal it. I borrowed it."

"Check your dictionary. Borrowing without permission *is* stealing."

"I don't argue definitions before morning coffee." She walked to the bed and grabbed the sheet, suddenly aware that the T-shirt and panties she had on covered very little of her body.

Ryder walked about the room, checking the bathroom and the closet for who knew what. Finally he leaned against the bedpost and stared at her. "I didn't come to argue definitions. Actually, I didn't come to find the truck, either."

"Then what did you come for?"

"Answers."

Simple enough, only the answers he wanted wouldn't be. And if she made the mistake of giving him the truth, there would be no way to stop Ryder from jumping on a bronc that wouldn't give up until he was as dead as—

As dead as Shawn. As dead as the man whose body they'd found last night. Her heart caved in to a mass of nothingness as she studied the hard jut of Ryder's jaw.

"Take the truck, Ryder, and go, while you still can."

"Is that a threat?"

She shuddered, wondering what, if anything, she could say would make him leave. She gave up. "Ask your questions, Ryder. I'll answer them if I can."

"Why didn't you tell me when you found out you were pregnant with my child?"

She exhaled sharply. That wasn't the question she'd expected. She tugged at the corner of the sheet she'd turned into a cloak, knotting it about her hands. "I was afraid you'd…" She ran her fingers through her hair as the lie died on her tongue and unshed tears moistened her eyes. She looked up and met his gaze. "I wanted to tell you."

"But you didn't. You just took your newborn daughter to a friend's house and left her with the boyfriend. Anything could have happened before she was placed in my care."

"You're not being fair, Ryder. I knew Kate would bring her to you as soon as she got home from work. I knew you'd take care of her, that your family would love her."

"We do. We all love her very much. Maybe that's why I can't understand why you don't."

His tone was hard, accusing. It cut through her resolve. "Is that what you think, Ryder, that I just dumped my baby girl because I didn't want to be bothered with her?"

"Are you saying I'm wrong?"

She tried to swallow her anger and hurt, but it swelled in her throat until she thought she'd die from suffocation. "I'm saying you don't know what love is until you've had to give up your child. You don't know how your heart can just break completely, how your arms can ache to hold her.''

The tears were coming now, fighting their way out of the corners of her eyes and sliding down her cheeks.

Ryder dropped to the bed beside her. He put his arms about her shoulders and pulled her close while sobs shook her body. She'd held it all in so long, and now that she'd broken down, she'd lost all control.

''Please go away, Ryder. Just leave. I'm begging you.''

''No.'' His hold on her grew all the stronger. ''I'm not going anywhere. Not until I know the whole truth. Not until I know who you're running from and why.''

She pulled away just far enough that she could look into his eyes. ''You'll hate me, Ryder.''

''The truth, Kathi. You've lived the lie too long.''

''You don't want to know. It will drag you into the same trouble that stalks me.''

''It already has. I'm a suspect in a murder case. Maybe two. Whoever it is that you're so afraid of had to be the man who followed you last night. He knows we were together, so whether you tell me the truth or not, he will assume that you did.''

''Why would he?''

''Give me another reason why he'd think you traveled to Kelman to talk to me.''

Her mind whirled, the result of too many pain-killers and too little sleep. And the situation she'd pulled Ryder into.

Ryder trailed a finger down her cheek. "I'm begging you, Kathi, for both our sakes and our daughter's, tell me what's going on. Give me a chance to defend myself and to keep you and Betsy safe."

She sighed. "I'm probably making the biggest mistake of my life, Ryder, but I can't fight you on this any longer. Take me out for coffee, and I'll tell you about the day Shawn Priest was murdered."

Chapter Six

Kathi warmed her hands around the paper coffee cup. She'd been a fool to think she could come into Ryder's life for even a moment of time without bringing the danger with her.

"Are you cold?" Ryder asked. "If you are, we can sit in the truck."

"No, the fresh air feels good." Especially after the stale air of the motel. She stretched her legs, and moved her foot to a more comfortable position, grateful that it didn't ache the way it had last night.

Morning coffee in the great outdoors. It was so like Ryder to suggest getting their coffees at a drive-through so that they could have their conversation at a roadside park instead of in a noisy café. He fit better in this space. Rugged, earthy, natural.

They sat across the concrete picnic table from each other, soaking up the first rays of early morning sun, treading gingerly along the unfamiliar edges of being together again. Finally she broke the silence. "How did you find me?"

"My brother Branson put out an APB on you as soon as Arlo called and said you'd taken the truck.

You managed to dodge the cops all day, but you left enough of a trail that I knew the general direction you were traveling in.''

"I purposely avoided leaving a trail. I kept to the back roads and only stopped when I had to."

"And you were *almost* successful."

"Where did I slip up?"

"The troopers handed out flyers we'd made using a photograph of you that I'd taken when we were...you know, together."

He'd avoided the word "lovers." The slight cut a little, but she understood it. She had been the one who'd walked away without a word. Sipping her coffee, she tried to force her mind to the issues at hand and away from feelings she shouldn't have. "So now my picture and description are posted in employee bathrooms and next to the cash register of every quick stop across Texas?"

"I'd say that pretty much covers it. A guy in Batesville reported that you'd gassed up at his place in the afternoon. A man in a truck stop in Loma Alta saw you later in the day. In both cases, it was the limp that had caught their attention." He lifted his gaze to meet hers. "But it was a woman named Marsha who nailed you down for me."

"Marsha?"

"The waitress at the truck stop where you'd stopped to grab a cola and go to the bathroom. She said you'd asked about a place to stay and she'd suggested the SunUp Inn."

Marsha the motormouth. Why was she not surprised? "I can't imagine that the state of Texas pursues all truck thieves this vigorously."

"No, but they do pursue murder suspects, and running made you appear a lot more guilty than you would have seemed if you'd just gone in and answered a few questions like I wanted you to do."

"I didn't kill that man down by the creek. I had nothing to do with that."

He turned his hands palm up. "I'm not the one you have to convince."

She grimaced and took another sip of her coffee. The brew had started to cool and the bitterness of it lingered on her tongue, an appropriate match for her feelings. A murder suspect. Just one more complication to an already hopeless situation.

She'd come a long way. Less than two years ago, she'd been young and carefree, madly in love with a sexy rodeo star. Her life had stretched in front of her like a ribbon of glittery satin, exciting and full of surprises.

Now, two deaths later, she was a hundred years older, a mother of a baby she didn't know, and a suspect in a murder case. All because of what she'd stumbled into on a morning very much like this one. She looked up to find Ryder staring at her, and the urge to walk around the table and slip into his arms was almost overpowering.

What sad irony. All this time and the only thing that hadn't changed was the way she felt about Ryder.

No. That had changed, as well. Grown complicated and twisted. Grown dangerous. "Why did *you* come after me, Ryder?"

"I just told you."

"No, I mean you personally. If you already had

every man in the state with a badge looking for me, why did you drive all night to find me?''

"That should be evident. I came because I need to know everything you do about Shawn Priest's murder.'' He pulled the defining Stetson lower over his forehead, shadowing his eyes and the strong lines of his face. "And unless I'm misreading the signs, I'd say you're about to be stomped into the dirt by a snorting bull.''

"Even if I am in danger, it's not your concern. Not anymore.''

"You're Betsy's mother. That makes it my concern.''

So that was it. He'd come running across Texas to find her because he thought he owed it to Betsy. It had nothing to do with her as a woman. Nothing to do with the nights they'd laughed and made love until the sun had pushed its way over the horizon. Still, she'd dragged him into the danger. She owed him the truth, at least as much of it as she dared tell him.

But she couldn't tell him everything. A few secrets had to stay hidden if she was to protect her daughter. And nothing mattered more than keeping Betsy safe.

"I'll tell you what I know, Ryder. I hope it helps.'' She closed her eyes for a second, forcing her mind to delve back into the shadows that ruled her life. "How much do you know about Shawn's past?''

"Not much. I know he worked for Kincaid's, that he'd been with the organization since a couple of years after he graduated from high school. He seemed to have worked his way up the ladder fairly quickly.''

"Shawn never graduated from high school. He was in and out of detention centers from the time he was twelve, and seriously hooked on drugs before he turned sixteen. Joshua Kincaid, the man who owns the nightclub chain, hired him himself, right out of a halfway house."

"Joshua Kincaid owns a ranch not far from ours. He and my dad grew up together."

"Well, luckily for Shawn, he saw something in him no one else had. The judge had warned him it was his last chance. The next time he was picked up on any charge, he was going to throw the book at him."

"Apparently the threat worked."

"I don't know." She guided her fingers up and down the strained muscles in her neck. "Shawn claimed that it was Joshua Kincaid who turned his life around. He gave him a job when no one else would."

"Ah, yes, that Joshua Kincaid is quite a man."

The sarcasm in his voice was obvious. "Do you know something I don't know about Mr. Kincaid?" she asked.

"You worked for him. You should know him better than I do."

"I respected him. He was always fair with me, and he's an excellent businessman. He kept his Texas-themed nightclubs making money when a lot of big-name clubs went broke after the urban-cowboy fad died."

"He knows how to make money. I'll give him that. I'm just not sure he always chooses the honest path."

"I've heard the rumors you're talking about, but I don't believe them. I never saw a sign of anything illegal in either of the clubs I worked in. And I know that he's helped a lot of guys like Shawn."

"So if Shawn was saved from a life of crime by his boss, what does his past have to do with anything now?"

She took a deep breath. She was stalling, but it would do no good. "I don't think Shawn had fully left his old life behind."

Ryder shook his head. "I'm not sure I know what you mean, but I can almost guarantee you that Shawn wasn't a user. He was impulsive, at times, a thrill-seeker. But he wasn't on drugs. He was too physically fit."

"Nonetheless, I think he was still involved with some of the guys he used to run with."

"Why? Did you see him with them?"

"I think so." She shuddered as the terrifying images haunted her mind. "And I think it was those friends who killed him."

RYDER GNAWED on the theory Kathi was dishing out. It was interesting, but it lacked substance. "Keep talking," he said. "Give me facts."

"Do you remember the weekend I flew to Tulsa to watch you compete?"

"I remember." He remembered too well. He'd come within a hair's breadth of asking her to marry him that weekend. He barely knew her and yet he wanted to be with her every second. He'd turned chicken at the last moment.

"I flew home on Sunday, right after the competition. When I got home, I had a message from Shawn. He sounded upset, desperate, but he didn't say why. I tried to return his call, but he wasn't home. I kept trying until midnight, never getting anything but his dreaded answering machine.''

"And you think he was already dead then?''

"No.''

Her voice dropped so low, he had to strain to hear her. She propped her elbows on the table and buried her head in her hands. A few seconds later, she lifted her head and met his gaze. "I woke up early that morning, before the sun. I tried to call Shawn again. The machine had been turned off, but there was no answer. I got dressed and drove over in the dark.''

"Why would you do that?''

"He was a friend. I thought he might need me.''

And that was the Kathi he remembered. The old longing surfaced, knotting in his gut. He forced it into submission before it made him do things he'd be sorry for later. Things like moving over to sit beside her and holding her trembling body in his arms.

"I saw his car when I drove up,'' she continued, "so I knew he was home. It was just getting light then. I opened the car door and sat there for a minute, wondering how I would explain to Shawn why I was knocking on his door at daybreak.''

"You could have just told him the truth, that you were worried about him.''

"That's what I decided. Only I never got the chance. Just as I opened the door, a strong gust of wind hit, tossing the dust and grit from the parking lot into a whirlwind. The sand blew into my eyes. It felt like ground glass in my contact lenses.''

He winced. "That must have stung."

"Like crazy. And that's when I saw Shawn racing across the parking lot with two pieces of luggage in tow." She crumpled the remains of the coffee cup in her hand. "I called to him, but he didn't even look my way."

Ryder started to interrupt, she held her hand up to silence him. "I rubbed my eyes, trying to clear them, and the right lens popped out and into my hand."

"Could you see if Shawn was with someone?"

"He was by himself. I called to him, but he didn't turn around. By then my left eye had started to burn and water so badly I couldn't see. I took the lens out and reached into my purse for my glasses, but I couldn't find them."

"And Shawn had still never acknowledged that you were there?"

"No, he just kept walking across the parking lot. I stepped out of my car to call to him again. But before I could, a black van drove up and two men stepped out. Shawn started to run back toward his apartment. A second later, Shawn fell to the concrete. One of the men must have shot him, but there was never a sound."

Kathi was white as a sheet now, her voice raspy. Ryder bounded around the table and pulled her into his arms. She clung to him, like a lost child who'd suddenly been found. He held her that way for long minutes, her tears wetting his neck.

"I watched Shawn being murdered in cold blood, and all I did was stand there. No, all I did was run.

I found my glasses in my purse, started the engine, and took off without a backward look.''

"Did you call the police?"

"I called 911, but I didn't give my name. I only told them that a man had been shot, and where."

"Then you did what you could."

"I did *nothing*. Don't you see? I did nothing but run to save my own neck."

"You couldn't have stopped them. You had no idea what they were going to do. And even if you'd tried, you would have only gotten killed yourself."

"Sometimes I wish I had."

"You don't mean that." Ryder held her close, rocking her to him until the sobs subsided. Finally she pulled away.

"Let's get out of here, Ryder. Let's drive, with the windows down so we can feel the wind."

He led her back to the truck. There were still questions in his mind, but they could wait. Kathi had already been to hell and back in the past two days. She had to be reaching her limits.

Her step was unsteady. Her ankle still swollen, though not nearly as much as it had been two nights before.

Two nights ago.

That was all it had been since she'd stepped through the door at the Roadhouse. It was hard to imagine that so many feelings could be compressed into such a short period of time.

She leaned against him as they made their way back to the truck. His arm was about her waist and the sense and smell of her invaded every part of him. Kathi was back. But this time, he'd make sure he knew what he was doing before he fell under her spell as completely as he'd done before.

He wasn't just a fun-loving rodeo jock this time around. He was a father.

THE MAN STOOD in the shade of a pecan tree, drinking bourbon-laced coffee from an insulated travel mug and watching the cowboy and the lady stroll back to the pickup. He pulled his light jacket closed and zipped it shut. The wind had a bite to it this morning, though Ryder Randolph and Kathi Sable didn't seem to notice.

His arm was locked around her waist, and she leaned into him, her eyes swollen from tears, her ankle from her narrow escape two nights ago.

Two nice young people who had stumbled into the middle of something that was none of their concern. Now they had to be taken out to protect the guilty. The guilty ran the world. Sad but true.

In his own mind, he never felt like one of the guilty, though he survived by doing their dirty work. He was a victim, just like Ryder and Kathi would be. And just like them, he'd stumbled into his predicament.

He turned and walked to the men's rest room as they got nearer. He doubted seriously they'd pay him much mind even if they'd had to step around him to get to Ryder's truck, but he wasn't one to take chances.

Not when he was this close to the kill.

He heard their footsteps behind him and felt the familiar twinges of regret. They were two people who had every right to live, and he was one man the world would never miss.

But he knew in the long run that he would be the one still breathing when all this was over.

BRANSON PACED the narrow sheriff's office. Ryder should be here any minute. Ryder and Kathi Sable. Betsy's mother. Funny, after all this time, it didn't seem Betsy *should* have a mother, especially not one he and the rest of the family had never met.

Betsy was Ryder's child, but mostly she was a Randolph, the first daughter born into the family in two generations. She'd won everybody's heart so completely that there wasn't a one of them who wouldn't go to the grave to protect her.

Betsy's mother had given her up, walked away without so much as a phone call to check on her. For a whole year, Kathi Sable hadn't cared two cents about her daughter. Now she was riding back into her daughter's life on a wave of trouble. He, for one, had never liked it one bit.

He liked it a whole lot less since he'd taken the phone call from the San Antonio forensics lab a minute ago. The man who had been murdered last night was no longer the unidentified victim. He was an off duty Fort Worth cop. A man without one reason for being in Kelman, Texas. But he had been here, in the spot that Kathi Sable had lured his brother to about the same time the man had been killed.

He only hoped Ryder hadn't been taken in again by this woman. Or worse, that Ryder wasn't still in love with her. A year ago, he'd thought love was just an illusion that men latched on to to keep them from feeling lonely. But that was before he'd met Lacy.

Now he knew just how real love was. He couldn't imagine life without Lacy—didn't even want to try. And if Ryder felt that way about Kathi, then Ryder was in for a backbreaking ride. They all would be.

He heard footsteps in the hall. He walked over, pulled open the door and got his first look at Betsy's mother. But all he really saw was Ryder's arm around her waist, protective and supportive. Trouble. Any way you sliced the pie.

KATHI TOOK Branson's hand when it was extended and managed to smile her way through the introductions. The moment was awkward, tense, fraught with distrust. None of the Randolphs had any reason to like her, and yet, according to Ryder, they were all hopelessly smitten with her daughter. If that mattered at all, you couldn't prove it by Branson's reception. His eyes were cool, his manner downright cold.

"Come on in and pull up a chair," Branson said. "This isn't official. I'm not involved in the investigation, but I have some questions that need answering—if you're willing to talk to me as Ryder's brother."

Ryder held his hat in his hands. "What do you mean you're not involved in the investigation?" Ryder asked.

"I was officially replaced today."

"Due to the fact that I'm a suspect in the murder, I guess."

"Among other things. Mostly because it's the second body in a week found on Randolph property."

Branson leaned his backside against his desk and toyed with a chrome pen. "At any rate, the rangers will be handling this case, as well as Shawn's murder. I was told that if they needed me, they'd let me know."

Ryder led Kathi across the room and pulled out a chair for her. "Any news on the last body?" he asked, resting his hands on the back of the chair as she sat down. "Do we know who it was?"

"As a matter of fact, we do. The body has been positively identified as belonging to Kent Quay, a Fort Worth cop."

Kathi's mouth went dry, and her insides felt suddenly queasy. Apparently Ryder noted her distress. He turned to face her.

"Do you know this man?"

"I'm not sure."

"What kind of answer is that?" Branson asked, his voice harsher than it needed to be.

"A truthful one."

Ryder stepped in between them. "Simmer down, Branson. Kathi came back to Kelman to help."

"Oh, so that's what she came back for. I thought perhaps it was just to help send her daughter's father to jail, or maybe get him shot."

His tone dripped with resentment. Who could blame him? It hadn't been her intention to cause trouble, but she'd done just that. "Look, Branson, you don't want me in Kelman, and I don't want to be here. I've already told Ryder what I know, so why don't you just get the rest of the story from him?"

Branson walked behind his desk and dropped into his chair. "Actually, I'd like to hear it from you."

"We'll do this any way Kathi wants," Ryder cut in. "I told you that on the phone. She's been through enough, and she doesn't need any static from our end."

"It's okay, Ryder. I'll answer his questions."

Branson nodded, his lips still tight. "I appreciate that. I apologize if I've misjudged you, but you have to admit you seem to attract trouble."

And that was the understatement of the year. She took a deep breath, scooted back in her chair and answered his questions, retelling the same painful story she'd gone through earlier with Ryder. Only Branson never even winced as she described the cold-blooded assassination of her friend. She suspected he'd heard much worse.

"Why didn't you go straight to the police station?" he asked.

"I don't know. Shock, I guess. Or maybe just fear. I went home. A little while later, a policeman knocked on my door. I told him what I'd seen and he left. That was the last I heard of any of this until I saw in the paper that Ryder was being questioned for Shawn's murder."

"You didn't call anyone, and yet a cop showed up at your apartment to question you about what you saw?"

"Right."

"How did he know you'd seen the murder?"

"I assumed they traced my 911 call."

"How did he react when you told him you were an eyewitness?"

"He asked me a lot of questions, wanted to know if I could identify the men who shot Shawn. I told him I couldn't because of the problem I had with my contact lenses."

"And he bought that?"

"No, Branson. Not at first. He was a cop, like you. He didn't call me a liar, but it was clear he didn't believe me. He thought I *had* seen the men, and was holding back from fear of retaliation."

And it was clear that Branson thought the same thing. But she had told Branson all she could. Any more, and Ryder would figure out the truth about why she'd walked away after his accident. He'd understand why she'd left her baby girl in his care, and he'd never let her walk away again.

"Let me see if I have this straight." Branson's eyes narrowed. "A cop came to your apartment to question you about the murder of your friend. You told him you were an eyewitness to the murder but that you couldn't identify the killers. And the cop left and never bothered to talk to you again."

"You've got it."

He picked up a yellow pencil and scribbled a few notes on a legal pad. When he finished, he tossed the pad back onto his desk and stared at her until she looked him in the eye. "There was no record of Shawn's murder, Kathi. How do you explain that?"

Kathi shifted uneasily. No matter how many times she lied, it never came easy. "I guess you should ask the Fort Worth cops that question."

"I plan to, but I think I know what their response will be. They'll insist that if someone had come out to question you about the murder, there would be a record of it. They'll say you're lying."

"Why would I?"

"You tell me." He stood and raked his fingers through his dark hair. "You might as well. One way or another, I intend to find out."

She was sure he wasn't bluffing. That's why she had to leave Kelman. Tomorrow at the latest. For Ryder's sake and especially for Betsy's.

"I've told you what I know, Branson. I certainly can't explain the actions or mistakes of the Fort Worth Police Department."

"Tell me again what the policeman said when he showed up at your apartment."

"Let it go, Branson." Ryder stepped behind her chair and put his hands on her shoulders. "She's been through enough today."

Branson threw up his hands in surrender. "Okay, it's your hide they're after."

"Right, and browbeating Kathi won't save it."

They went through the motions of a polite farewell. Branson was trying, but he clearly didn't believe her. He was giving up for the day, but he wasn't about to let her story lie. His priority was keeping his brother out of jail.

Ryder was lucky to have him on his side.

Right now she'd just like to know if Kent Quay was the cop who'd come to her house the day Shawn Priest was murdered. And if he was, then who had killed him, and why.

"What about my car, Branson? Can I pick it up now?"

"It's been taken in as evidence. You'll have to talk to someone with the Texas Rangers about how to get it back."

"Am I free to leave town?"

"As far as I know, but the Rangers may have other thoughts on the matter."

"Since they haven't told me differently, I'll assume I'm free to catch a bus out of town." She turned on her heel and walked to the truck while Ryder and his brother talked a little more.

"It's way past lunchtime," Ryder said, joining her at the curb. He jerked the door open and held it while she climbed in. "Are you hungry?"

"I could probably eat a salad," she said, after he climbed behind the wheel and turned the key in the ignition. "Then I'd like a ride to the bus station."

"I know a spot where you can get the best home cooking this side of the Mississippi River. And maybe a salad, too."

"Is it somewhere close by?"

"A few miles out of town, but it's worth the drive."

"Does this fantastic place have a name?"

"Yeah. We call it the Burning Pear. And while we're there, you can meet your daughter."

THE TENSION in the truck grew so thick Ryder couldn't have cut it with a silver spur. His offer had stunned Kathi into silence. To tell the truth, he wasn't sure where it had come from himself. He only knew that Kathi was not the uncaring monster he'd made her out to be in his mind. He also knew that whatever had driven her to abandon Betsy was still driving her.

He started the engine and pulled the truck onto the highway that ran through town, the same one that led to the Burning Pear. He started in that direction.

Kathi held on to the silence, her body rigid in the seat next to him.

Finally she stretched, rubbing her hands on the rough denim that covered her thighs. "I can't go to the Burning Pear, Ryder." Her voice was strained, as if someone had forcefully pulled the words from her throat.

"Why not?"

"You saw how Branson reacted to me. There's no reason to think the rest of your family will feel any differently."

"We're not going there to visit my family. Besides, there's probably no one there this time of the afternoon except Mom and Betsy. And possibly Branson's wife, Lacy."

"What about your brothers and their families?"

"Dillon and his wife and son have their own place on the ranch, just down the road from the big house. Actually, they wouldn't be there anyway. Dillon's giving a speech in Corpus Christi tonight, and Ashley and Petey drove over there with him. My brother Langley and his wife live on a neighboring ranch that she inherited from her uncle. They moved into their new house last month."

"What makes you think your mother would want me there?"

"Even if she didn't, you'd never know it. She'd never be inhospitable to a guest."

"Not even one who abandoned her grandchild?"

"Not unless she thought you'd come to take Betsy away." He slowed, pulling across the center lane to pass a slow-moving tractor. Old Ben Cousins going from one field to another. He waved and Ben waved back.

He checked his rearview mirror. Ben noticed and tipped his hat, probably wondering who Kathi was. He'd undoubtedly know soon enough. Around here, gossip ranked right under high-school football as the major form of entertainment.

Another car was behind Ben, evidently driving at the same speed as Ryder. He'd noticed it a few miles back, and it hadn't gained on him or fallen behind. He speeded up.

Kathi shifted in her seat, turning to face him. "Is this the way to the bus stop?"

"No."

"Then turn around now."

He kept going. "What's it going to take for you to stop pretending that *our* daughter doesn't exist?"

She knotted her hands into tight fists. "Just take me to the bus stop, and forget you ever knew me. I'm not the person you think I am, and I don't want to visit Betsy."

Her words slashed into him like jagged glass. When she'd walked out of his life nearly two years ago, he'd been devastated, hurt and angry at the same time. But now she was rejecting their daughter, and the pain was a hundred times worse.

"What do I tell Betsy when she gets old enough to ask what happened to her mother?" he said, not bothering to bite back the resentment.

"Just tell her that..." Her voice broke. Pulling a tissue from her pocket, she held it to her eyes.

A knot swelled in his throat. He slowed the truck, pulled onto the shoulder and parked. "You're right,

Kathi. I don't know why you abandoned Betsy. Maybe I wouldn't understand if I did, but it's your decision.''

"Just take care of her, Ryder. Take care of my baby girl.''

Turning, he rested his arm on the back of the seat. His fingers touched the silky strands of her hair. His insides melted.

"Kathi…I can help.''

She shook her head. "I'm…I'm just not ready to face the responsibility of a family.''

An unfamiliar car passed him. They were getting more and more strangers around here lately. Time was when he knew every person that passed him on the road. Back then, a murder would have been unheard of. Even now, it was a rare enough occurrence to have everybody in town talking—everybody except Kathi.

"Why did you come here in disguise?'' He cursed under his breath. He was doing it again, pushing her when it was clear she wanted no part of him, sticking his heart on a stake that was about to be hammered into the ground.

"I was protecting myself, Ryder. I was afraid that if I showed up in Kelman and was seen talking to you, the cops might decide they should hold and question me in Shawn's murder, as well. I was his friend, too, remember.''

"But still you came to tell me what you knew.''

"Does that surprise you so much?''

"Nothing surprises me anymore.'' He dropped his arm from the back of the seat. "There's not all that many busses through Kelman. I don't even know if you can get one out today.''

"No bus. No car. This is not the most convenient of towns to leave.''

"It's not all that convenient when you're staying, either.'' He turned the key, and the truck's engine purred to life. He was about to pull onto the road, when he noticed the blur moving toward them, a car traveling well over the speed limit. It slowed as it came closer and he caught sight of an object stuck out the window.

He sprang to action, shoving Kathi to the seat and falling over her as the sound of gunfire blasted away the quiet.

Chapter Seven

Bullets ricocheted off the hood and side of the truck and shattered the windshield. Quick and dirty, and then the black sedan roared past them. Ryder straightened, thankful he'd felt no wallops of pain. "Are you all right?" he asked, giving Kathi a quick once-over.

"Yes." Her voice was scratchy, her breathing quick and shallow. "How about you?"

"As okay as a man can be who just had a barrage of bullets whiz by his skull."

She peered into the darkness where the car had disappeared. "We've got to get out of here," she murmured. "Now, before he comes back."

Ryder brushed a sprinkling of glass from her shoulder. "Never a dull moment when you're around. That's for sure."

She groaned. "I told you you were better off without me."

"You told me a lot of things. Too bad you omitted the most important one, like who's trying to kill you."

She glanced around nervously. "Just drive, Ryder. Take me into town and drop me off. I'll disappear."

"Disappear into a grave like Shawn Priest did or just vanish the way you have for the past two years?"

She closed her eyes, suddenly dizzy and nauseous as the numbing effects of shock gave way to reality. The stalker who had been a step behind her for months had caught up. "Please, Ryder. No questions. I just need to get out of Kelman."

"I'm calling someone to pick us up. If we go down the highway in my truck, we'll have a face full of sharp glass from that shattered windshield. It needs to be scraped and new glass installed."

"And while we're waiting around for a ride, we may both get killed."

"By the man who's *not* chasing you? The danger you're *not* in."

"Okay, I lied. I'm in trouble, but it doesn't concern you."

"It does now. Someone just took a few shots at me, and that makes it my concern."

He put in a call on his cell phone to Branson. She waited beside him, her head spinning. For nearly two years, she'd exercised constant caution, watched her back, lived behind closed doors and drawn curtains. But at least she'd managed to keep the danger centered on her. Now it was spiraling out of control. Her head dropped forward, and she rocked it in her hands.

"Branson's on his way," Ryder said as he clicked off the phone. "He'll be here in minutes, and we're not exactly unprotected in the meantime. I have a gun and I know how to use it. I've shot holes in a lot of tin cans while I've been waiting around for my knee to heal.''

He took her hand. Strong. Protective. She closed her eyes and drifted back to a night long ago. He was holding her close, dancing, laughing. A lifetime ago. So why couldn't her heart and mind forget?

RYDER PACED Arlo's small kitchen. Kathi was in the guest room, resting her ankle. She had refused to go to the Burning Pear. And under the circumstances, he wasn't going to leave her alone in the motel in Kelman. So Arlo's was the only logical choice. ''I really appreciate your letting Kathi stay here after she stole your truck.''

''Well, she can't steal it again. I don't have it back yet.''

''I could run you up there to pick it up tomorrow.''

''Langley's already offered. Besides, it looks like you'll have your hands full here.'' Arlo ran a clean cloth along the slide handle of the shotgun he was cleaning. ''So Kathi still hasn't told you why someone's trying to kill her?''

''As far as she's concerned, it's none of my business. She wants me out of her life. She's made it perfectly clear that she doesn't need or want my help.''

''If she wanted you out of her life, she wouldn't have come back to Kelman.''

Ryder mulled over Arlo's response. ''So why do you think she's unwilling to talk?''

''You know her better than I do, but from my experience in law enforcement, I'd say it's one of three things. Either she's out to frame you, she's afraid you're one of the bad guys, or she's trying to protect you.''

"She's not out to frame me.'' Ryder stopped pacing and dropped to a chair. "If I hadn't thrown her to the seat when I did today, she'd have likely taken a bullet to the right temple.''

"And if she was afraid of you,'' Arlo said, "she wouldn't be here. You just saved her life. Looks like that leaves number three.''

"My gut reaction to all of this was that the men knew she'd seen them and were after her. But if that's the case, wouldn't she have just gone to the police for protection? Or even come to me. She knew I wouldn't turn her down.''

"Maybe she *was* coming to you—the day you were injured in the hit-and-run accident.''

A string of mild curses escaped Ryder's lips. Of course, Arlo was right. He should have put it together the second Kathi had told him that she'd seen Shawn murdered. She hadn't just walked away from him then, she'd run for her life. And she'd been running ever since. She'd risked her own life to come back now to tell him what she knew.

"Thanks for hitting me over the head. Next time I'm that dense, just use a baseball bat.''

"You're not dense. You're personally involved, and that always clouds the judgment. Keep that in mind every time you talk to Kathi Sable.''

"You don't trust her, either, do you? Even though you think she's trying to protect me.''

"I trust her motives. I'm just not sure I buy her story.''

"You don't think she really saw Shawn murdered?"

"She may or may not have seen it. I'm just not sure I believe she doesn't know who did it, or that she actually told the police what she knew. But I'm sure Branson is going to want her to visit the morgue and see if she recognizes the cop who was killed at the campgrounds the other night."

"Yeah, he mentioned that when he drove us over here after the drive-by shooting incident." Ryder drummed his fingers on the bare oak table. "I'm sure this is all tied in with why she won't have anything to do with Betsy, but I don't understand how she can be this near her own daughter and not even want to see her."

"I guess you'll have to get that answer from her."

"She hasn't even asked to see a snapshot of Betsy."

"Not all women have that mothering instinct the way your mom does, Ryder. Be careful you don't read qualities into Kathi that you wish were there." Arlo took his cleaned and reloaded shotgun and carried it to the gun rack. "It seems strange to be giving advice about women to Ryder Randolph, but here goes. Keep your heart out of this. Murder is serious enough without adding emotion into the formula."

Ryder nodded, but he knew it was too late to take Arlo's advice. His heart had never been uninvolved with Kathi Sable, not from the day he'd met her.

"I think I'll go in and check on her."

"You mean confront her, don't you?" Arlo said.

"If she's doing this to protect me, I want to know

it. And I want it to stop. If there's any protecting to be done, I want to be the one doing it.''

"If you need backup, I'm right behind you."

"Thanks."

"In the meantime, I think I'll open a few cans of chili.''

"Chili comes in cans?"

"Yeah, bud. This is not the Burning Pear.''

Ryder walked down the hall to the bedroom. He pushed the door open a crack. Kathi was spread out on the bed, her hair tousled, her eyes closed, her breathing slow and easy. He tiptoed over and pulled the sheet and light blanket up to her chin. She looked so peaceful, like the Kathi of old. His heart turned inside his chest.

"Your running is over," he whispered. "Your daughter needs you. And so does her dad.''

KATHI STRETCHED and opened her eyes. The room was gray, shadowy and cold. Fear stirred inside her, dissolving slowly as she remembered where she was. Her mind felt numb, as if she'd slept for days. A door creaked open and a rectangle of light illuminated her room, finding new shadows to play across her bed.

"Ryder?"

"Yeah, it's just me. I didn't know if you were awake. You were sleeping soundly the last time I peeked in.''

"What time is it?"

"Four o'clock, or close to it.''

"In the morning?"

"Yes. You slept right through dinner. I figured you needed the rest. How's the ankle?"

She moved her legs beneath the covers. "Better. Much better."

He stepped over and sat beside her on the bed. The worn mattress slumped under his weight, and she had to brace herself to keep from rolling into him.

"Why didn't you tell me what was going on months ago, Kathi? What made you think you had to fight this thing alone?"

"I don't know what you're talking about."

"You know exactly what I'm talking about. If I hadn't been such a dumb jerk, I would have figured it out on my own. I would have at least known that you had a good reason for running out on me." He took her hand in his. "Instead, I wallowed in resentment, convinced myself that you were just another buckle bunny, interested in me only as long as I was riding the roughest bronc and chalking up the most points."

"You quitting the rodeo had nothing to do with me leaving. Neither did Shawn's murder." The lie was shaky on her lips. He would pick now to question her about motives, when she was still groggy from sleep. Her throat was scratchy, dry. She picked up the glass of water from the table by her bed and took a few swallows.

"So why did you walk out on me, Kathi?"

"It seemed like the time to move on."

"I don't believe you. I think you left because the men you saw that morning at Shawn Priest's house think you can identify them. I think they've threatened you. Now they've tried to kill you—or have they tried before? Is that what started you running?''

She lay still. Her senses were suddenly razor-sharp. She could feel her heart beating in her chest, hear the sounds of Ryder's breathing, taste the bitter fear that she'd lived with so long.

The one thing that had kept her going for the past year was the knowledge that Betsy was protected from danger. Her daughter lived in a fairytale world surrounded by a loving Texas family and wide-open spaces untainted by fear. She had the best daddy in all the world to take care of her.

All that would come to an end if Ryder jumped into the bottomless pit with her. ''Please, Ryder. Just stay out of this.''

''What kind of man would I be if I did?''

''A live one.'' She lifted herself on her left elbow. ''You can't do this to your family. You can't do this to *our* daughter. If they think you know what I know, you won't have another minute's peace. If you walk down the street with Betsy in your arms, she'll be a target. If you take her for a ride and a sniper shoots at you the way that guy did this afternoon, she might take the bullet.'' Her teeth were grinding, her jaw so tight she could barely talk. But Ryder had to listen to reason. ''I gave Betsy up rather than put her in harm's way, and I won't let you place her there now.''

''Betsy will be safe. I promise you that.''

''Are you willing to give up your life, to spend your days and nights in hiding?''

''Absolutely not. I'm ready to put an end to this, and I'll do whatever it takes to make sure these men never bother you again. How could I face Betsy if I did anything less? I couldn't even face myself.''

"And if we're both killed, Ryder. Then what happens to Betsy?''

"If we died, Betsy would be the most loved orphan in the world. She's got three doting uncles, three aunts, a cousin and a grandma who adore her.'' He stood. "But that's not going to happen. So try to go back to sleep for a while longer. You'll need it. We have a couple of killers to stop.''

She watched him walk away. He was the Ryder of old. Cocky. Self-assured. Sexy. She just hoped he knew what he was up against, because she certainly did.

LANGLEY WALKED into Arlo's kitchen and set a couple of brown grocery bags on the counter. Ryder watched as Langley unloaded his haul. Croissants, fresh-squeezed orange juice, slices of baked ham, homemade blackberry jam and a tin of homemade cookies.

"We weren't going to starve to death, Langley. Arlo has the basics.''

"These go way above and beyond the basics. Besides, you know how Danielle loves to cook. We could feed the entire population of Kelman with the food we have on hand.''

"Won't Danielle miss this stuff?''

"She's the one who packed it.''

Ryder felt a constriction in his chest. He had to walk a fine line until he knew exactly what was going on and who was involved. "I asked you to keep the fact that we were staying at Arlo's a secret.''

"I don't keep secrets from my wife. If I tried, she'd see right through me." He opened the freezer and stuck a couple of wrapped packages inside. "But don't worry about Danielle. She understands the consequences. I just hope you do. I don't want this to spill over to the Burning Pear."

"I wouldn't do anything to put the family in danger, but I can't just throw Betsy's mother back to the wolves."

"Is that how you're rationalizing this?"

"What does that mean?"

"Is it Betsy you're worried about or have you just never gotten over Kathi Sable?"

Ryder raked his hands through his hair, shoving it away from his forehead. "I don't really know how I feel about Kathi right now. The only thing I'm sure of is that I can't turn away from her as long as she's in danger."

"I just hope you know what you're doing."

"Well, let me assure you that I don't. I feel like a blind man running through a cow pasture. No matter where I put my foot down, it'll probably be in a fresh pile of something that stinks."

He spooned a heaping helping of grounds into the ancient coffeemaker. "There's so many firsts—my first time to be questioned in a murder case, first time to be shot at, and definitely my first time to serve as a bodyguard."

"And your first time to go into hiding." Langley took the last of supplies from the sack and then pulled out a kitchen chair. "I can understand how you feel about doing what's right, but I think you should just go to the cops, turn this over to them and let them put Kathi in protective custody.''

"Before I do that, I want to find out why she didn't go to them originally. She's a smart woman. She had to have a good reason to run.''

"I'm behind you in this, Ryder. A man can't just ignore his child's mother if she needs help, but Branson's real uneasy.''

"That's nothing new. He's never admitted that I grew up.''

"I don't know about that, but his theory is that Kathi ran because she's not totally innocent in all of this.''

"Did he tell you that?''

"Not in those exact words, but he's convinced she knows more than she's telling. If she and Shawn were in something together, and he got caught, that might explain why she ran.''

"You can tell Sheriff Branson Randolph that he's dead wrong.''

Ryder jerked around at the sound of Kathi's voice. She was standing behind him, leaning against the door frame, pale, but her eyes were bright and slinging fiery daggers. "What else has the good sheriff said?''

Both Ryder and Langley wisely kept silent.

KATHI'S BARE FEET slapped the cold tiles as she stepped into the kitchen, and the draft from the open back door seemed to travel right through the shirt of Ryder's that she'd found lying in the chair beside her bed.

She stared at the cowboy who'd voiced the sheriff's theory. He had some of the same rugged features as Ryder, but his hair was blond where Ryder's was dark, and his nose was straighter, more classic.

He stood, but stared right back. Thankfully, Ryder's shirt hung low enough to cover all her private parts. She fumbled with the buttons she'd missed and finger-combed her short hair.

"Kathi Sable, I presume."

"That's right."

"And this is my brother, Langley." Ryder walked over to stand beside her. "He came by to deliver breakfast and to pick up Arlo. He's taking him back to the motel to get his truck."

"And Arlo's anxious to get going," Langley said. He picked up his hat, stuck it on his head and then tipped it to Kathi. "Good to meet you. Now I know where Betsy got her good looks. Of course, we knew all the time it wasn't from Ryder."

He walked to the door and stopped. "I'll give Branson your message," he said, "but he tends to be a Missourian Texan. He's a lot more 'show me' than 'tell me'." He grinned. "But you'll win him over. Any mother of Betsy's can't be all bad."

"Thanks. I think."

"I'll walk out with you," Ryder said, following Langley to the back door.

Kathi watched as the two men strode toward Langley's truck, both with the same easy, relaxed gait that defied the fact that Ryder had likely joined her on someone's hit list. Now that he was sleeping with the enemy, or at least under the same roof as her, the killers would assume he knew everything she did.

And he did. Or didn't, because they both knew exactly nothing about the identity of the killers.

Leaving the back door, she walked over to examine the oven. The white enamel was chipped, the surface streaked with scratches. It looked as if it predated electricity, but evidently not. It responded to her touch. A red light popped on and the oven began to heat.

Freshly baked croissants, family support, a hometown where everyone knew and respected you. That was Ryder's world. Suspicion, danger around every corner, death. That was hers.

Now the two were one.

IT WAS MIDMORNING on a beautiful spring day. The birds were singing overhead, acres of bluebonnets nodded in the breeze and she and Ryder sat perched on the railing of Arlo's porch. In this setting, she could have almost forgotten that she lived in chaos. Ryder made certain she didn't.

He droned on like a persistent mosquito, going over and over what she'd already told him. "Tell me again about the policeman's visit."

"I was home, sick to my stomach and shaking, trying to get my wits together enough to call the police. I know your brother Branson didn't believe me when I told him that, but it's the truth."

"Don't worry about Branson. He thinks like a lawman. Actually he did even before he became one, but he's fair and he never backs away from trouble. And once he's sure he's right, he'll go after something with all he's got."

"He's right now. He thinks I'm causing trouble for you."

"You're not holding a gun on me. I'm here because I choose to be." He leaned against the support post and propped his booted foot on the porch railing. "How long was it from the time you got back home from Shawn's apartment until the policeman arrived?"

"It seemed like a few minutes. It could have been as much as an hour."

"Did he tell you about Shawn's body being found, or did you mention it first?"

She shook her head. "I don't remember."

"Try. It's important."

She couldn't see why, but she closed her eyes and tried to recreate the scene in her mind. She remembered the cop well, could have drawn his face from memory, but she couldn't recall the exact sequence of the conversation. Funny how some things were marked indelibly in her memory and others had never been more than fuzzy images.

"I can't remember, Ryder. In the state I was in, I probably just blurted everything out. But he knew about the shooting. He told me Shawn was dead. I do remember that much. He was nice. He didn't seem upset that I hadn't come to him."

"How do you know that? What did he say?"

She bit back a groan. "I don't remember the conversation word-for-word. It was almost two years ago."

"Just try to remember what he said about getting back in touch with you."

"I am trying. As best I can remember, he said

something to the effect that I was not to worry. He would take care of all the reports. Oh, and I do remember one other thing. He told me not to mention Shawn's death to anyone at work."

"Didn't that strike you as a strange thing to say?"

"Everything about that day was strange. I was still dealing with the shock and grief. I just assumed he wanted the benefit of surprise when he questioned people."

"Apparently you followed his advice to the letter. You didn't even call me." A tinge of hurt crept into his voice. "Why didn't you call me, Kathi? You knew I'd want to know."

"How could I call you? You were dashing all over Oklahoma, making two rodeos that day, trying to pick up as many points as you could. I didn't have a clue as to how to reach you."

"I drove back to Fort Worth the next day. You sat right next to me all through lunch and never once told me that one of my best friends was dead."

She could hear the anguish in his voice. But it was no worse than the anguish she'd dealt with every day for months. But she couldn't go on like this, and there was no need to anyway, now that Ryder knew she'd left to protect him.

"Okay, Ryder. You want to know everything, I'll tell you everything. I had a phone call that night from a man I didn't know. He asked me to meet him in a bar on the other side of town. I don't know why I went except that he sounded so desperate to talk to me, and he said it had something to do with Shawn's death."

"What happened?"

"When I stepped out of the car, a masked man grabbed me from behind. He told me to get out of town, to disappear completely if I wanted to live. If I went to the cops or if I told anyone what I'd witnessed, I'd get the same thing Shawn had."

"And based on that, you ran, without even talking to the cops."

"I called them. The officer I spoke with didn't have a clue what I was talking about. He said he had no record of a shooting at the address I gave him. That's when I knew that the cops were in on this. I didn't know how, but I knew they were."

"But you didn't take off at once. You had lunch with me the next day."

"To tell you goodbye." Her breath burned in her lungs. It was as if it were happening all over again. The death. The pain. "I had planned to tell you that I was moving on, that you meant nothing to me, only I couldn't. I wasn't strong enough to say the words. So I just walked away." Tears burned at the corners of her eyes. She tried to blink them away.

Ryder stepped beside her and circled her waist with his arm. "Why didn't you just tell me the truth, Kathi? Surely you trusted me."

"I trusted you." She looked away. "And I cared too much about you to pull you into this."

"Don't you think that should have been my decision?"

"No, especially not after I saw that car plow into you." She shuddered but met his gaze. "That wasn't an accident, Ryder. And I'd already seen one friend shot down in cold blood. I knew what these men were capable of, and I couldn't let that happen to you."

"So you ran without even telling me I was going to be a father."

"I ran without even knowing it. I ran the minute I knew you were going to be all right. And I never stopped running until I saw in the paper that you were being questioned in Shawn's death."

"You walked back into danger to help me."

"Only it didn't help. I made a terrible mistake."

Ryder pulled her into his arms. Just as he had so many nights in her dreams. She clung to him, her head on his chest, her arms locked around him. All wrong, and yet it felt so right.

He tilted her chin with his thumb. "I'm glad you're here, Kathi. And nothing will ever make me sorry that you came back." And then his lips found hers.

Chapter Eight

Ryder went weak. He hadn't meant to kiss Kathi, but he couldn't help himself. Now, when a million questions should claim his attention, all he could think about was the feel of his lips on hers, the curves of her body as she clung to him.

She kissed him back, hard, her lips parting and inviting. His body ached with the same cravings that used to drive him nearly mad. The months of resentment dropped away, and it was like she'd never left him.

Her hands explored his back with quick, intense strokes and then slow, deliberate ones that seared right through the thin fabric of his shirt. He could feel her heart beating against his chest, feel the heat of her breath mingling with his.

It had been so long since he'd held her like this, yet he knew her body by heart. Remembered the soft mounds of her beautiful breasts, the delicate crevices below them, the sweet, hot slickness of her when he touched her in private places. He knew and the knowing made him want her all the more.

His lips left hers to probe and fondle the smooth

lines of her neck. Need consumed him, made him clumsy and awkward on one hand, driven on the other. His fingers fumbled with the buttons of her blouse, releasing them one by one until the fabric pulled open.

He kissed and nibbled his way across her flesh, nudging her breasts until the nipples peeked over the lacy edge of her bra. The tips were pink and pebbled, even more perfect than he remembered. He wrapped his mouth around one exquisite nipple while his hands circled her tiny waist.

She moaned with pleasure, arching her body toward him. But then her body went rigid. She released a shaky breath and pulled away. "We can't do this, Ryder. We can't just go back to where we were."

It took a minute for his brain to react to her words. His body still couldn't. "Are you saying you didn't like what we were doing, because it sure seemed like you did."

"No." She met his gaze. Her eyes were misty, soft as a newborn doe's, but not nearly as trusting. "I could kiss you, could make love to you, but it wouldn't be right. Not the way things are now."

"You'll have to do better than that, Kathi. Explain to me how things are, because I obviously have them confused. I understood you to just say that you walked out of my life to protect me and that you walked back into danger in order to help me. You didn't say anything about falling out of love with me. Or were you only lying all the times you said that you were?"

"I never lied about that." She trembled and looked away. "But that was months ago. The whole world has changed since then. We can't pretend it hasn't.''

"We could if we feel the same.''

"But we don't. We can't. We're not the same people we were then.''

"I'm still Ryder Randolph. I don't ride broncs, but believe me, I'm still a man.''

"Maybe you haven't changed, Ryder, but I have. I've lived a lifetime in the past two years. I'm not the fun-loving woman that used to swoon over you at the rodeo.''

"I never thought you would be.'' He dropped her hands and she stepped away from him. He was hurt, bewildered, and still he wanted her. "Is there someone else?''

"No, of course not. How could there be when I've been afraid to even make a friend? I would never have dragged anyone into my horrid life. Afraid to step outside the door in the morning and more afraid to step back in at night.''

He looked away from her, stared at the acres of dirt, grass and cactus that stretched beyond Arlo's porch. The land around him hadn't changed, probably wouldn't in his lifetime, at least not so much you'd ever notice. Maybe that's what bound so many men to the flat South Texas landscape. You could depend on it. Apparently that wasn't true with women.

Kathi touched his arm. "I'm sorry, Ryder. I didn't mean to hurt you. Not when I walked away from you in Fort Worth, and not now. I didn't plan any of this.''

He tugged his hat lower, a habit of his when he

wanted to block out the world. It never worked and especially not in this instance. "So what will it be, Kathi? We can talk, but not kiss? Touch, but not intimately? Sleep under the same roof, but not together? Put our lives on the line to stop a killer, but not make love? Are those your ground rules?"

"You make me sound unreasonable. That's not the way it is, Ryder. I'm not trying to be difficult."

"Neither am I. I just like to know where I stand."

"I care for you, Ryder. I'm not going to lie and say that I don't. But I don't even know myself any longer. And right now there's no time for me to find out who I am."

She was right, of course. He'd listened to his body and his heart. He'd believed that she would do the same. No matter how bad other things were, he still needed the closeness they'd once shared, or maybe needed it more because of the danger.

But she was making rational judgments, protecting herself. He'd always known she was a very smart woman. She'd proved it yet again. "I'm going inside," he said, turning away from her. "I need to make a few phone calls."

"Do they have to do with the murder case?"

"You told me the first night that Shawn had two good friends who might know something about why he was killed. Branson has tracked down Julia Rodrigue. She's living just south of Fort Worth, but Bull seems to have vanished. The best he could do in that area was Bull's brother. I'm going to see if either or both of them will talk to me."

"See if they'll talk to *us*. We're in this together now. If you go to Fort Worth, I'm going with you."

She stood and walked toward the front door. "And I've been thinking more about the man who was killed the other night at the campground."

"What about him?"

"I'd like to see the body. There's a chance I might recognize him. It could be the same cop who came to my apartment right after Shawn was murdered."

"Branson and I have already talked about that, but you won't have to go to the morgue. He's coming over this afternoon and bringing snapshots that were taken at the crime scene."

"A visit from Sheriff Branson Randolph." She groaned. "Makes a visit to the morgue seem like a vacation."

MARY RANDOLPH SAT on the floor watching Betsy play with her plastic nesting cups. The little darling was really good at stacking them into a tower and at fitting them inside one another. Bright as sunshine on a barn roof she was, just like her dad had been.

"Da-da-da-da-da."

"That's right. You're just as agile and clever as your dad was when he was your size."

Betsy tired of stacking her cups and picked one up and threw it. It bumped and jiggled along the wooden floor, and she broke into sweet baby laughter. She started to crawl after the bright red cup, but changed her mind.

Instead, she used Mary's arm and shoulder to pull herself up. "Horsey," she said, or at least a close approximation of the word, as she toddled to the handmade rocking horse.

She wasn't quite big enough to mount the carved

horse, but she liked to stand there and make it rock, and she loved to pull on its fake mane. The same way all Mary's boys had. The same way her grandson Petey had until only a few months ago.

Betsy was a Randolph. She belonged here on the land that had been in the Randolph family for generations. She needed them, but not nearly as much as Mary needed her granddaughter. With each son after Dillon, she'd prayed secretly for a daughter, never once letting her husband know how badly she wanted a girl.

But each time a son was born, she forgot all of that. Each of her boys was different, and yet every one of them had carved out his own niche in her life. Petey had done the same. Theirs had been a family of men.

Only now there was Betsy, the first Randolph girl in two generations. Mary planned to live a very long time. She'd see Betsy get baptized at the church, dress for her first prom, graduate from high school and then college and finally waltz down the aisle to become some lucky man's wife.

The phone rang. Mary walked to the desk in the corner and picked up the receiver.

"Hello."

"Mary, this is Debbie Griffith. I had to call you and see how you were holding up under the new developments."

"I'm hanging in there." Barely, and even though Debbie and her husband were family friends and she did most of her shopping in their department store, she was too heartsick to talk about Ryder's problems to anyone. "Ryder is totally innocent," she said, hoping Debbie would get the hint. "I have to believe things will work out."

"I didn't mean with Ryder. I meant, how are you standing up to Betsy's mother showing up in Kelman after all this time?"

Mary gripped the receiver a little harder. "There must be some mistake."

"You mean she's not in town? I'm glad to know that. I heard she was here and she'd come to get her daughter. I couldn't believe the nerve of a woman who'd abandon her own child and then show up a year later, expecting to take custody of her."

"Who told you Betsy's mother was in Kelman?"

"Someone mentioned it in the store. But, if it's not true, I won't worry."

But now Mary was really worried. If what Debbie said was true, that would explain the whispered conversations that stopped when she stepped into a room. She'd thought they were shielding her from talk about the investigation, but they might have been protecting her from the truth about Betsy's mother.

"Let me call you back, Debbie. Branson came home for lunch and he's still around. I think I need to talk to my sheriff son."

"Now don't go getting upset with Branson. I told you, it was probably just unfounded gossip that I heard."

"That's okay. I'm about to find out if it's founded or not." Mary hung up the phone and picked up Betsy. Her pulse raced crazily as she stormed down the hall. Obviously, there were more holes than one in the fence. She stepped to the door that led into the hallway.

"Branson Taylor Randolph. I need to talk to you."

BRANSON EXHALED sharply. He knew the tone, the same way he knew what it meant when his mother called him by his full name. She was extremely displeased with him. And this time he had a good idea what had drawn her ire. He met her in the kitchen, the suitcase full of clothes and the album that he had packed for Ryder in hand.

"I'd like to know why I have to hear from Debbie Griffith concerning what's going on in my own family."

Good old Debbie. "What did you hear?"

"That Betsy's mother is in town and that she's come to take custody of her daughter."

Branson took his mother's hand. He could feel the veins through her thin skin. It struck him that she was growing older, that it was only familiarity that made him think of her as the same young woman who had ruled over him and his brothers when they were growing up.

He had already told his mother about the body found at the campground. He'd even told her that Ryder had been out there with a lady friend the night before. That was the kind of news you couldn't keep secret in a town like Kelman. But he and his brothers had decided not to tell her that the lady in question was Betsy's mother, unless Kathi decided that she wanted to see her daughter. And they definitely didn't want to explain that someone had fired on Ryder and Kathi the other night.

"Kathi Sable *is* in town," he said. "She's with Ryder now, but she's not here to claim Betsy."

Her eyebrows arched, and she stared at him suspiciously. "Then why is she here?"

"She was a friend of Shawn Priest's and when she heard about Ryder being questioned in the murder, she wanted to see if she could help him."

"How could she help? Does she know something?"

"She knows the names of some of Shawn's friends up in Fort Worth. I'm going to help Ryder track them down."

Betsy grabbed at Branson's arm. He reached over and swooped her into his arms and onto his shoulders. "She's not interested in taking Betsy away with her," he said, giving his mom what he hoped was a reassuring smile. "So you can put your mind at ease."

But Mary Randolph didn't smile back. "I don't understand. What kind of woman is this? She's right here in town, and she hasn't come out here to see her own child?"

"Don't ask me to explain it. All I know is she's planning to leave town right away—without Betsy."

At the sound of her own name, Betsy started wiggling. Branson took her from his shoulders and swung her over his head.

"Mo. Mo." The baby gurgled.

"That's the trouble with you women. You always want more." He swung her a few more times and then returned her to the floor. She lifted her hands to him again. "Sorry, pumpkin, your uncle Branson has to go back to work."

Mary eyed the suitcase. "Lacy didn't say anything about your leaving town."

"That's because I'm not. The strap's broken on it. I'm going to get Elmo to have a look at it. If he can fix harnesses, he should be able to fix a luggage strap."

Mary followed him to the door. "Where's Ryder now?"

"I told you. He's talking to Betsy's mother."

"Did he talk to her all night? He didn't come home."

He threw up his hands. "He's staying with Arlo, just like he told you on the phone. And that's all I know. I'm not his keeper. He's a big boy, Mom. He can take care of himself."

"I'm not so sure about that."

"I am. Now don't worry. If he can't take care of himself, then I'll stick my nose into his business."

"Is that a promise?"

"It's a promise." He bent and kissed her cheek.

MARY PICKED Betsy up and held her in her arms as she watched Branson drive away. The cloud of dust lingered long after he'd disappeared. She wasn't sure what was going on, but she knew that Branson had not told her the whole truth.

And if he couldn't tell her the truth, then something was dreadfully wrong.

BRANSON COULDN'T REMEMBER having ever lied to his mother before—not even when he was a kid. He wouldn't have done it now if there had been any other way. But if she knew the kind of danger Ryder was flirting with, she'd go out of her mind with worry.

And they didn't need anyone else to worry. He was doing enough of that already. If he'd known the other night what he did now, he'd have set up a roadblock and never let Kathi Sable cross the town limits. He didn't know if she was telling the truth or not, but any way Ryder ran his horse, he'd be looking a rattlesnake in the eye.

Kathi Sable was a walking target for a desperate killer and his little brother had just jumped in front of her. And nothing Branson said seemed to be getting through to him. Ryder had said he was doing it all for Betsy, but after one look at him and Kathi together, Branson knew it was more than that. Ryder was still in love with her. And love could make a man do crazy things.

Branson himself was living proof of that. He reached for his phone and punched in the number of his wife's cell phone. She was in San Antonio for a doctor's appointment today, but he had a sudden craving to hear her voice.

KATHI STEPPED outside the front door of the cabin and walked down the steps and toward a faded bench that sat twenty yards or so from the house. Her ankle was much better today, although she was still staying off of it as much as possible. But now the desire to escape Arlo's dark cabin outweighed her need to keep the strain off her ankle.

Ryder had been on his cell phone for ages, calling people Shawn had worked with in Fort Worth, trying to find someone who knew anything. She'd supplied him with the names, but she didn't expect him to have much luck. There was a big turnover in the nightclub business, and even if some of the same people were still working at Kincaid's, she doubted they'd know anything about Shawn.

He'd had few friends at work, preferring to spend his leisure hours alone or with friends she'd never met. But he had never mentioned having trouble with any of them.

So why had two men shown up at dawn one morning to blow him away? And why had the police never investigated the murder?

Get out of town. Tonight. Don't trust the police. They can't help you. Talk and you're next. You and your cowboy lover.

The warning she'd gotten that night rang in her ears. She walked away from the house, toward a shady spot beneath a cluster of mesquite. The wind made a crinkling noise in the leaves, and a buzzard circled overhead. She stood watching as he surveyed the area and then landed in a patch of thick grass a few yards beyond.

Shawn, if you had just said something in that message you left me to let me know who was after you. If you had given me a name or a reason. Or if I had just gone to work that morning like I had every other morning for the past few years instead of going by to check on you....

Footsteps fell in the grass behind her. Her breath caught, as if someone had cut off her air supply. She turned, but it was only Arlo walking toward her. She'd been so caught up in her thoughts, she hadn't seen him drive up.

"If you're looking for Ryder, he's in the house."

"I'm not looking for Ryder."

"What do you want with me?"

"Not *with* you. It's what do I want *from* you."

"Okay, I'll bite. What do you want from me?"

"I want you to stop playing games and level with Ryder."

He stepped closer, and her nerves skidded crazily. "I don't know what you're talking about, Arlo."

"Who's paying you to set Ryder up?"

She backed away, hating the accusing look in Arlo's eyes. "I came here to help Ryder," she said. "You know that."

"No, what I know is that you led him out to the Larker place on the pretense that you wanted to talk, and then a killer showed up. If he hadn't been detained by a flat, he might have been the one killed instead of that cop."

"I didn't lead him to the Larker place. It was his suggestion that we go there."

"I think you know who killed Shawn Priest." His voice was rough, threatening.

"How could I know? I told you and Branson and everyone else who asked that I didn't have my contact lenses in. I couldn't see the men's faces."

"You also said you received a warning. That's a little farfetched in my mind. If the kind of men who executed Shawn wanted you dead, you'd be six feet under right now, or swimming with the fishes. In my book, that means your story is a lie."

"You're wrong, Arlo."

"I hope so, for your sake." He didn't seem convinced. "What kind of relationship did you have with Joshua Kincaid?"

She didn't like his innuendos. Arlo wasn't a cop

and he wasn't one of Ryder's brothers. He had no right asking her any questions at all. "Joshua Kincaid was my boss. And I didn't play footsies at the office, if that's what you're getting at."

"Why not? You're Joshua's type. Young and pretty."

"I was Ryder's type. I was dating him."

"So I've heard." Arlo's stare softened a little. "And I hope it was because you liked him and not because your boss wanted him set up."

The accusation was confusing. She started toward the house and then stopped. "Why would you think Joshua Kincaid might want to frame Ryder for murder?"

"Because Joshua Kincaid has friends in low places, the kind of friends who've been known to hire men to make the same kind of visit that Shawn received."

"Shawn and Joshua Kincaid were good friends."

"Sometimes friendship, like love, goes sour."

"I'd need a lot more than bitter quips to believe that of Joshua Kincaid."

"I hope you're right, but the fact is, someone killed Shawn Priest and a Fort Worth cop. I don't have a thing in the world against you personally, but I don't want to see Ryder go to jail."

"I don't, either, Arlo. Believe me, I don't."

He walked beside her as she started back to the house. "Forgive me if I came on too strong back there. It's just that I'm damned worried about Ryder. Now let's go inside. I have some news that both you and Ryder might find very interesting."

Arlo's booted feet crushed the grass beneath his

weight. Their shadows stretched in front of them, his large enough to swallow hers.

Arlo had no reason to worry about her. The last thing she'd ever do was deliberately hurt Ryder. And she had never been involved in anything that included murder.

A truck roared down the drive to Arlo's cabin. She watched as it skidded to a stop and Branson jumped out.

The gang was all here. She was in for another fun afternoon.

RYDER HAD MADE up his mind to listen to everything Branson and Arlo had to say, but he'd also made up his mind that they were going to do this his way. Branson wouldn't like it, but it was Ryder's call.

Arlo stood in front of the hearth, the fingers of his right hand curled around a cold beer. "Shawn Priest's murder had nothing to do with anyone's drug turf. He wasn't using at the time, and he hadn't crossed any kingpin's path."

Branson propped one hand against the oak mantel. "How did you find that out?"

"I still have a few connections on the street."

Ryder buried his hands deep in his pockets. "So where does that leave us?"

"At the end of a dead-end street," Branson explained. "If it had been a drug execution, we'd have some clues as to who might want Kathi dead. As it is, it could have been anyone Shawn ever ticked off."

"Anyone capable of shooting a man in cold blood," Arlo added.

"Or with the funds to have him killed." Branson turned his gaze on Kathi. "You worked with Shawn. Did he ever mention any kind of trouble that he was in? Did he owe someone large sums of money or did they owe him?"

"I wouldn't know about any of that. Shawn seldom talked that much about himself. At least not to me."

"Did you know any of his friends that weren't from work?" Branson asked.

"No, but then I had only been in Fort Worth six months. Before that I was office manager at the San Antonio club. The only friends I remember hearing Shawn mention were the two I told Ryder about, and I never actually met them. From what Shawn said, they seemed more like ex-friends."

Branson's mouth screwed into a scowl. "Ex-friends are a good place to start."

Ryder let the conversation replay in his mind. He wasn't a cop, didn't have the training Branson and Arlo did, but he'd known Shawn. He liked to act tough, but he wasn't the mean kind. But something had been going on at work, even if Kathi hadn't been aware of it. Shawn had been ready to walk away from his job. He'd even talked to Ryder about traveling the rodeo circuit.

So who had killed him and gotten away with it? And why had the cop who'd come to Kathi's apartment not reported the murder? And why in the hell had they buried him on Randolph property?

"Somehow this has to all go back to the cop who came to Kathi's apartment," Ryder said.

"If he really *was* a cop." Branson rattled the keys

in his pocket. "It's not that hard to pick up a uniform and a fake ID. He could have done that to keep Kathi from reporting the murder. Then they could dispose of the body without anyone even knowing he'd been killed."

Arlo ran his hand over the edge of the mantel. "*If* Kathi remembers all of this accurately."

"I remember," she said.

"But you don't remember if the cop's name was Kent Quay," Arlo said.

"I was in shock. I had just witnessed my friend's murder, and the cop's name wasn't high on my priority list."

Ryder walked over and stood behind her, planting his hands on her shoulders. "We're just trying to make sure we have all the angles, Kathi. No one blames you for any of this."

"*You* don't blame me. I'm not sure that's true of everyone here. But we could answer one question now if Branson brought the picture of Kent Quay with him."

"I have it right here." Branson walked to the coffee table and picked up a manila envelope. He took out three snapshots and handed them to Kathi.

Ryder watched as she examined each one, and he knew the answer before she finished.

"This is him. This is the man who asked me all the questions about what I'd seen that day." She dropped the pictures to the table. "What do I do now?"

"You talk to the ranger who's heading up the investigation. Tell them everything you've told us.

What you saw that morning. What Kent Quay said when he showed up at your house.''

"Will that clear Ryder?"

"It all depends on whether or not the guy believes you."

Ryder touched a hand to her shoulder. "Why wouldn't he believe her?"

"Because it's twenty-one months after the fact, and because her ex-boyfriend needs her testimony."

"So my coming back here to testify as to what I saw that morning may not do any good at all?"

"I didn't say that," Branson said. "It's going to be valuable to Ryder's case. It just may not be enough to convince the rangers. They'll weigh your motivation for coming up with this story so late in the game."

Frustration piled on top of frustration. "I didn't come up with the story late. I reported it on the day of the murder."

"And that will be your word against the Fort Worth Police Department. And now the one cop who could supposedly back up your story is dead. I'm sure the rangers will find this an interesting scenario."

"I'm flying to Fort Worth tomorrow," Ryder said. "That's where the answers are."

"I'll go with you," Branson said.

"No. The minute you walk in, people see a cop. When I walk in, they just see a friend of Shawn's who's in trouble. They're a lot more likely to open up to me."

"I don't recommend it," Branson said.

"I know." He put a hand on Branson's shoulder.

"And I appreciate your wanting to help. But I'd like to do this on my own."

"And what about Kathi?" Arlo asked. "Will she be staying here at my place?"

"No," Kathi answered for herself. "I'm going with Ryder."

"You're dealing with a cold-blooded murderer," Branson said, his mouth drawn into thin, fighting lines. "There are two bodies to attest to that fact."

"And I'm just trying to make sure there's not a third."

FINALLY BRANSON LEFT and Arlo went out to tend to a few afternoon ranching duties. Ryder picked up the suitcase Branson had brought over and threw it onto the bed. Jeans, shirts, underwear, shaving supplies—everything he'd asked for.

And the album. He reached down and pulled it from beneath the stack of folded clothes. Hoping he wasn't making a big mistake, he slid the book under his arm and walked into the kitchen where Kathi was rummaging through the packages of frozen food Langley had delivered earlier.

"You might be interested in this," he said, placing the album on the table and opening it to the first page and the first picture they'd ever taken of Betsy. "It's a great book, titled *Watching Betsy Grow.*"

She walked over and glanced down at the book. One look and he could see the change in her stance, the slump of her shoulders, the tired tilt of her neck. When she turned back to face him, there were tears in her eyes. Trembling, she sank to a chair in front of the open album.

Chapter Nine

Kathi started to turn the pages in the neatly kept book of photographs. Her heart twisted inside her until it was all she could do not to scream in pain. The first year of Betsy's life lay captured in front of her, two-dimensional yet so real she could almost hear the laughter. Her baby, but she was not in the pictures with her. She had not rocked her to sleep or hushed her cries. It was the Randolphs who had shared those first precious months. They were the people Betsy knew, the people she loved.

She turned another page, her fingers trembling. In picture after picture, the adorable infant was surrounded by Ryder and her three cowboy uncles. In their arms, lifting her tiny fingers to touch their rough faces, smiling at their antics, wrapping her pudgy arms around their necks.

The emptiness swelled, turned her inside out, left her so hollow, she thought her bones might collapse in a pool of nothingness. She held her stomach, nursing the ache, knowing that nothing would ever make up for the year she'd lost with Betsy.

And yet she'd be eternally grateful for Ryder and

his family. They had given her baby a home and showered her with love.

"Tell me about the pictures, Ryder."

He drew up a chair and sat beside her. He didn't touch her, and yet she felt his presence as powerfully as if he'd taken her in his arms. Strange, he wasn't the happy-go-lucky cowboy she'd fallen in love with a lifetime ago; she wasn't the same impressionable young woman. And yet some illogical, invisible tether seemed to bind them together more strongly than ever before.

Perhaps it was their daughter. Or maybe their short affair had gone much deeper than the dizzying roller-coaster ride that had swept her off her feet and left her pregnant with Betsy.

Pregnant, alone and afraid.

"Which picture do you want to know about?" Ryder's voice startled her, though he was only responding to her question.

"Start with this one." She pointed to one where an older lady cuddled Betsy in her arms. Beneath the picture, someone had written in perfect script, "Babies are God's most precious gifts, given to grandmothers to turn the agony of growing old into a blessing."

Ryder tapped his index finger against the album. "That's Mom and Betsy. She could quiet her when none of the rest of us could. I swear the woman can cure the colic with the touch of her hands."

"Who wrote the caption?"

"Mom. She did all the writing in the book. She's the poet among us, though Langley comes up with some great limericks from time to time. Not *always* repeatable in mixed company, but creative.''

"Betsy looks so content in your mother's arms.''

"She should. She was there enough. Mom spoils her. Betsy loves attention, but she doesn't whine or anything if you put her down with her toys. Of course, she does cry if Petey tries to go outside without her.''

"Is that the cousin you mentioned?''

"Right. My older brother Dillon and his wife Ashley's boy. Petey is almost five, a ring-tailed tooter if there ever was one.''

He thumbed to the next page and found a snapshot to prove his point. Petey was perched on a low limb of a pecan tree. Betsy was in Ryder's arms, holding her arms out to Petey, obviously hoping he'd take her onto the limb with him.

"And here's one of Langley in action.'' He pointed out a picture of Langley, dressed in a western shirt, jeans and cowboy boots giving Betsy a bottle.

"Do all your brothers help take care of her? Does no one complain that it's women's work?''

"That question will be answered when you meet my mom. She runs an equal-opportunity household, has ever since we were youngsters.''

"I like that woman.''

Ryder turned the page and zeroed in on another snapshot. "Now this was a proud moment. Branson in it up to his elbows.'' The caption underneath the picture read: "Uncle Branson changes his first dirty diaper.''

Branson didn't look particularly pleased, Kathi decided. Score one for Betsy.

Ryder walked her through the rest of the pages, his face beaming as he described each of Betsy's accomplishments. The first time she rolled over, her first word: Da-da. Her first step. It was all documented in pictures and the loving words of Mary Randolph.

Color snapshots, Kodak moments, as the saying goes. All she could share of the first year of her baby girl's life. The experiences themselves were forever lost, stolen away by heartless killers. And now the evil had reached to the Randolphs, invaded Betsy's world.

Ryder would never run the way she had. He'd already started to fight back, dig into the past, find out things that would make him the same kind of target she'd become. She'd been a fool to think she could change any of that by coming back to Texas.

The memories of the past fused with the helplessness of the present. Anger stirred inside her and then swelled until she could feel it exploding in her chest. She'd run for almost two years. She'd be running still if it would keep Betsy safe, but now the danger had moved into Kelman. Her muscles tightened. Her determination hardened to solid rock.

''We can't let anyone hurt Betsy.'' She looked up. Ryder was staring at her, his eyes challenging.

''*We?* Does this mean you're not going to steal another vehicle and run out on me the second my back is turned?''

She thought about it, wanting to tell him the truth. ''I guess it does.'' She gulped in an unsteady breath. ''I'm not afraid to fight, Ryder. Not for myself. But I have to know that Betsy is safe.''

"Surely you know I'd never do anything to put her in danger."

"Not willingly, but you haven't lived with the fear that I have these past months. You didn't see Shawn Priest shot down in cold blood. I want to stop these men, but if going after them means dragging Betsy into harm's way, I'd rather live the rest of my life on the run."

He took her hand in his. "If we don't stop these men, the rest of your life, and probably what's left of mine, isn't worth a sack of moldy feed."

"I don't care. Just promise me you can keep Betsy safe."

"Betsy is my daughter, too, Kathi." His voice was intense, his eyes dark and embracing. "I'd go to the grave to protect her." He traced a finger down her cheek, and the searing heat of his touch, attacked the frigid walls around her heart. "And, just so you'll know. I'd go to the grave to protect you, as well."

Kathi pulled away. She shouldn't go there, shouldn't even try to deal with her feelings for Ryder in the midst of all that was happening. And yet the question persisted. "Why would you risk your life for me, Ryder? Is it because I'm Betsy's mother?"

"Partly." He stood and walked away from her, stopping to stand in front of the window. He stared into space for long minutes before he turned back to face her. Their gazes met and held. "You insisted earlier today that we didn't know each other," he said, "that the time we've been apart has changed us."

"I have changed. So much so I hardly know myself sometimes. I can't expect you to know me."

"Maybe I don't. But I know my own feelings. They haven't changed, not where you're concerned. I thought they had. I wanted desperately to forget you when you walked out on me. And then, later, I tried to hate you for abandoning our baby girl. But even then, when I had no idea why you'd left either of us, I could never hate you."

She rose and walked over to stand beside him. "I was right, Ryder, about both of us. We have changed. You're not the sexy rodeo jock I fell in love with. You're all grown-up."

"I guess becoming a father does that to a guy."

"Not all guys." She stepped closer, unsure of her feelings and yet overwhelmed by them. "You've turned into quite a man."

"All grown-up. And no longer sexy?"

"Oh, no. More sexy than ever." Far more sexy. She'd never been more aware of that than when she'd looked through the photographs. "Nothing is more seductive than a masculine cowboy rocking his baby girl to sleep or wiping mashed peas and carrots from her red cheeks."

"And from her hair, and from underneath her chin, and occasionally out of her eyes. And mine."

He was smiling now, but the tension between them hadn't diminished. The room crackled with it, the space between them as electrified as if lightning had struck.

"So where does that leave us, Kathi?"

"With a murderous secret to uncover and a couple of killers to track down." She knew that wasn't what he meant, but she dared not go beyond that.

She and Ryder were two weeks in the sunshine,

fourteen nights in the moonlight. They were laughing, dancing, and making love until dawn. But their two weeks had come to an abrupt end, and no matter how they tried, they'd never be those two people again. But maybe, when this was over, they'd get a chance to find out if the people they were now had a chance of making it together.

"I'll start dinner," she said. "Unless you think Arlo will mind."

"Arlo will love it. Even he can't stand his own cooking." He ambled over to the counter. "Are you sure you want to stand on that ankle long enough to cook? You've already been on it a lot today."

"Not so much, except when I walked outside for a few minutes. And in spite of the ugly bruise, it really is much better."

"Then you cook and I'll make airline reservations. I'll make them for the afternoon. Branson thinks one of the rangers will want to question you in the morning."

"And I get to tell the gruesome story all over again."

"It's necessary."

"I know. It's necessary even if they don't believe me. Then I'll be ready to fly out of here. Who do we see first?"

"Julia Rodrigue *Ferran.*"

"She's married?"

"As of a few weeks ago. It took her a while to agree to see us, but she finally gave in. I got the feeling while talking to her that her husband doesn't want her involved in this murder case in any way."

"I can't say that I blame him for that."

Kathi pulled out a sack of potatoes and started to peel a few for stew. "Once we start this, Ryder, I don't think there will be any backing out."

"There already isn't." He touched a hand to the small of her back. "But don't worry. I plan to win."

THE MORNING WENT worse than Kathi expected, if that was possible. Not only was it clear that the ranger did not believe her testimony, he insinuated that she and Ryder might have been working together in Kent Quay's murder. No matter that there was no motivation for Ryder to have killed Shawn in the first place and no explanation for why the cop had wound up in Kelman.

And the biggest mystery of all still centered around the question of why Shawn Priest's body had been buried at the Burning Pear.

By the time they'd reached the home of Julia Rodrigue Ferran, Kathi was already disgruntled and discouraged. Still, she was impressed with the neighborhood.

"Looks like Julia did well for herself," she said as they stopped at a brick guardhouse. A uniformed woman stepped out and asked if one of the residents was expecting them. When Ryder said yes and gave his name, the guard checked her list and finally looked at them as if they were part of the human race.

"Your names are on the approved visitor list," she said. "Have you been to the Ferran home before?"

"No, ma'am, can't say that I have." Ryder exaggerated his drawl and flashed her a smile.

The woman flushed, instantly transformed. It was

the cowboy charm, Kathi decided. No woman was immune, not even one who could have passed for an automated robot a few seconds ago.

She offered them a map of the neighborhood and took her time explaining to Ryder just which turns he should take. Kathi barely listened. Her attention was on the houses that dotted the hilly landscape.

They were a bit too pretentious for her tastes, but they were impressive. If any one of them had come in at under ten thousand square feet, she'd be surprised. The grounds were equally ostentatious, stretching out forever, manicured to perfection, and professionally landscaped. No self-respecting weed would have been caught dead here.

She craned her neck to get a glimpse of a mansion that hid behind a privacy fence and a line of leafy trees. "If I'd known we were visiting the habitats of the rich and famous, I'd have dressed the part."

"I did. I have on clean jeans, and my next-to-best pair of boots."

"The guard was impressed."

"Something tells me Julia won't be. Not with the jeans or with the reason for our visit."

"Why did you tell her we were coming?"

"I told her that we were friends of Shawn Priest's, and that you desperately needed to talk to her."

"You didn't tell her I had seen him get shot, did you?"

"Of course not, but as soon as I said my name she knew that his body had been found on our ranch."

Kathi strained to get a better look at a mansion they'd passed. "So she had heard that he was dead."

"I think all of Texas has. What is it they say about finding fame in death?"

"That's the kind of fame I can do without. But Julia must have been upset to hear that Shawn was murdered. I mean they lived together for a long time. She had to care for him then."

"A man would like to think that. Did Shawn ever say who broke off the engagement?"

"No, but I'm sure she did. It was obvious from comments he made that he was still in love with her."

Ryder slowed to check the address on a California-style stucco house that spread out like a small town. "Maybe she just wanted more than what Shawn could offer. He couldn't have given her all this, unless he'd robbed a bank, won the lottery or both." He turned onto the winding drive.

Kathi let loose with a low whistle. "This looks like a Texas Taj Mahal. What does Mr. Ferran do for a living?"

"Squanders an inheritance, would be my guess. Her husband is Peyton Ferran III, grandson of *the* Peyton Ferran. He was one of the richest oilmen in the state when he died a couple of years ago."

"Did Julia tell you that?"

"No. I did my homework. Not that it was difficult. There aren't so many multibillionaires you can't keep track of them. Not even in Texas."

As soon as Ryder turned off the ignition, she opened her door and stepped outside. The camera at the corner of the garage swiveled as if by magic, responding to movement. "Smile for the camera."

Ryder did, and then tipped his Stetson. "You

never know where one of those snapshots will show up, especially when you're about to be arrested for murder.''

"Don't even joke about that, Ryder."

"I wasn't."

ONE LOOK at Julia Rodrigue, and Ryder knew exactly what had drawn both Shawn and Peyton Ferran to her. Words like *exotic, seductive* and *mystical* sprang to mind. Her hair was black, straight and shiny, the thick strands falling below her waist. She had on little makeup except around her eyes. They were shadowed in something that made them appear the color and consistency of wet emeralds. The silk shirt whose collar framed her face was a creamy white.

She was not smiling.

"Mrs. Ferran, I'm Ryder Randolph and this is Kathi Sable. I hope we're not too late. We hit a bit of traffic."

"You can come in," she said, "but I don't have long to visit. I'm expecting my husband home soon." She led them through a marble foyer and into the kind of room that made a man feel he should take off his shoes before he dirtied the carpet and stick his hands in his pockets before he broke something he couldn't afford to pay for.

"Your home is beautiful," Kathi said. "You have exquisite taste."

"Actually Peyton does. The house was already furnished before we were married." She talked in a soft, lyrical voice, one that matched her slow, graceful movements and walk. Ryder tried to imagine her having a beer with Kathi, Shawn and him in one of the neighborhood bars where they used to go to unwind. He couldn't.

"Have a seat," she said, motioning to a low-slung white sofa laden with pillows. "I'll have the housekeeper bring us some coffee, or would you prefer tea?"

They assured her coffee was fine. When she left, Kathi scooted closer. "Shawn had said she was beautiful, but I didn't expect her to look so—"

"So kept?"

"Is that how you think she looks?"

"Yeah. I get the feeling she's one of Peyton Ferran's possessions, like his expensive house and impeccable furnishings. Not that she isn't a knockout."

"So you did notice."

"I'm not blind. You're not jealous, are you?"

"Of course not."

Only he got the impression that she was, at least a little. And he liked that. Not that she had any reason to be. He'd be about as comfortable with a woman like Julia as he would be with a cobra. They were intriguing, too, but deadly.

Kathi walked over to a glass-fronted curio cabinet against the far wall. After a minute's scrutiny of some crystal boxes, she picked up a silver-framed photograph from the top of the cabinet. Her finger brushed the edge of an enameled music box as she did. The jar triggered a few chords of a familiar song he couldn't quite place. Kathi hummed along as she studied the photograph.

"I guess this is the happy couple."

Ryder walked over for a better look. Peyton was younger than he'd expected, with a good build. Both he and Julia were dressed in tennis gear and holding racquets.

"He looks familiar," Kathi said, "but I don't know why he would."

"Maybe you've seen his picture in the paper."

"Possibly, but I'm not a big fan of the society section. Still, I'm almost sure I've seen him somewhere."

"No doubt." Julia walked up behind them. "My husband gets around." She took the picture and set it back in place. "So, tell me, what is it that you need to ask me about Shawn?"

Ryder put a hand to Kathi's elbow and led her back to the couch. "We were both good friends of Shawn's."

"Then I'm surprised we never met."

Kathi crossed her legs, careful not to kick the spindly legs of the ornate coffee table. "We met him after the two of you broke up."

"I see. You were friends. And yet, the newspaper reported that Mr. Randolph had been questioned in his murder."

"I didn't kill him, if that's what you're worried about," Ryder said.

"Neither did I." Julia spread her fingers, showing off her fake nails and a diamond so big it could have slept in its own bunk. "Shawn and I had broken up long before he was killed."

"So you know the date of Shawn's murder?"

"No, but Shawn and I broke up almost two years ago, and I know Shawn was alive then."

Kathi uncrossed her legs and leaned forward. "Look, Julia, I know it probably seems strange for us to show up here when you don't know either of us, but I know how close the two of you were. Shawn told me what a wonderful relationship you shared.''

Ryder watched the change come over Julia. The muscles in her face relaxed, her eyes warmed. Evidently he'd put her on the defensive with his questions, but Kathi had struck some kind of chord.

Julia picked up a pillow, cuddling it in her lap as if it were a small puppy. ''What did Shawn say about me?''

''That you were beautiful and smart. That he'd never met anyone like you. That he'd fallen in love with you the first time he met you.''

''That was Shawn.''

She dismissed the claim with a wave of her hand, but Ryder could tell from her tone and expression that she was pleased Shawn had told Kathi so much about her. But, knowing Shawn, he doubted he'd put it quite as eloquently as Kathi had.

''What happened between the two of you?'' Ryder asked, trying to adopt Kathi's friendlier tone.

She shook her head, a sadness finally touching and softening her eyes. ''Mostly Shawn happened. He was impetuous and romantic, but also extremely undependable. I never knew when he'd be out of town, could never count on him to keep a date. His excuse was always that something came up. Only those somethings never had a name. I always suspected they were about five foot five and blond.''

''I don't think so,'' Ryder said. ''I think that those somethings he couldn't talk about were what got him killed.''

"Why would you think that? He never had an enemy, at least not one that I knew about."

Ryder leaned forward. "It's an exceptional man who doesn't have any enemies."

"Shawn was exceptional in many ways."

"I agree, but that doesn't mean he couldn't have gotten mixed up in something dangerous. Maybe his problems were connected to his work. Did he ever talk about his job?"

"All the time. He loved it."

"And did he also love his boss?"

"Joshua Kincaid? He practically worshiped the man. Mr. Kincaid gave him a job when no one else would take a chance on him. He said he'd probably be in prison if Joshua hadn't given him a job when he did."

Interesting. Shawn had apparently loved his job when he'd been with Julia, but that wasn't the story he'd given Ryder. All he'd ever heard was that Shawn wanted to start fresh in something that had nothing to do with nightclubs.

"Did he say why he thought he'd be in prison?"

"No, but I know he ran with a rough crowd before I knew him. He admitted that he'd experimented with drugs in high school. When he was caught with them on campus, he was kicked out. He never went back. He just returned to the house where he lived with his foster parents, packed up his things and hit the road. At least that's the story he told me."

"I didn't know he was in foster care. What happened to his parents?"

"His mother died when he was quite young—cancer, I think. His dad drank himself out of the picture.

The courts took Shawn when he was only ten and put him in foster care. I think Joshua was the closest thing to family he had.''

She stopped talking as the housekeeper came in with the coffee. She waited until the woman had left the room and they'd all taken their cups before she said anything else.

Julia took a deep breath. "I've never told anyone this, not even my husband. And he won't like it that I'm telling you."

"It's important that we know everything you can tell us," Ryder urged.

Kathi set her cup back on the tray. The sound seemed to reverberate from the ceilings and bounce off the crystal chandelier. "If you know anything at all, Julia, please tell us. The killer is still out there, walking around free."

"There are lots of killers out there, walking around free. But I guess it won't hurt to tell you this. I got a phone call from Shawn one night around midnight. He'd been drinking and his voice was shaky. He told me he was in over his head, but he didn't say what he was in. Mostly he just rambled. Said something to the effect that he'd thought he could leave anytime, but he'd been wrong."

"Thought he could leave what?" Kathi asked.

"He didn't say."

Ryder took a pen and small pad from his pocket. "Did he mention any names?"

"No. I asked him who he was talking about, but he said it was better not to know. He said he was just calling to say goodbye."

Ryder felt his insides tightening. They were finally

getting somewhere. "Did he say where he was going?"

Julia shook her head. "All he said was that he was leaving town and that he wouldn't be back. If anyone called looking for him, I was to tell them that he'd gone to visit his brother in Scotland."

Kathi fingered the necklace around her neck. "But you just said he didn't have any family."

"He didn't. That's why I knew he was in trouble."

"What night was that?" Kathi asked.

"August 9th. My birthday. That's why I remember the date."

And the tenth was the morning that Kathi had watched while two men approached Shawn, and one blew him into the next world.

The rest of the visit went quickly. Once Julia had eased her conscience by telling them about the phone call, she was anxious for them to go. Evidently, she was not eager to become embroiled in a murder case.

Ryder knew exactly how she felt.

THEY HAD BARELY cleared the guardhouse when Ryder's cell phone rang.

"Ryder Randolph."

"Ryder, I'm glad I caught you."

"I might be, too, if I knew who I was talking to."

"Joshua Kincaid. I know that you and Kathi Sable are in town. It just happens that I'm in town, too, planning some renovations to the local club. I was hoping you'd join me for a late dinner there."

Alarms went off in Ryder's head. "How could you possibly know that Kathi and I are in town, Kincaid?"

"Julia Ferran just called me. She said you came to her house to ask about Shawn Priest."

"Why would she call you?"

"Her husband and I are good friends, and she knows that Shawn worked for me. She thinks I might be able to help you. I think I can, too. Actually, I've been meaning to call ever since I heard that you'd been questioned in Shawn's murder."

"Why didn't you, if you thought you could help?"

"I doubted your brother Dillon would want my help, and at the time, I never thought your connection to the murder would go beyond questioning."

"And now you do?"

"Your name was mentioned in the Fort Worth paper again this morning as being a suspect. It was reported that your arrest was imminent."

Great. Too bad the police couldn't be as diligent at catching the real killer as they were at trying to get something on him. Ryder did need to talk to Joshua Kincaid, but he hadn't planned on a social visit. Still, now was better than later. And they should be safe enough in a public place.

"What time would you like for us to meet you?"

"Is eight too late?"

"Eight would be fine."

He said his goodbyes and broke the connection.

"What happens at eight?" Kathi asked, when he'd put away the phone.

"Dinner with your former boss. It appears he and Julia are phone pals."

THE MAN FOLLOWED a few blocks behind the rental car. Ryder Randolph and Kathi Sable. Together again. It was amazing. She could have been home free, but instead she came running back to the bronc rider.

Nothing had worked out according to plan. Nothing, not even the finding of the body. Now Ryder was digging and clawing into Shawn's death. He would never give up until he discovered the truth.

Or until he was dead. He and Kathi Sable.

The light turned from yellow to red. The man slammed on his breaks. He'd have to be more careful. The last thing he needed was to be arrested for running a stupid red light. Reaching into his jacket pocket, he wrapped his fingers around the vial of pills.

He twisted the top off and shook two of the capsules into his hand. He downed them both without water. They stuck in his throat, but he swallowed until they finally worked their way down his esophagus and into his stomach.

Someone honked behind him. He looked up. The light had turned green. He gestured to the man behind him and planted his foot on the accelerator. He had a car to locate, had to find out if Ryder and Kathi were staying in town or going back to Kelman.

Tonight might be a good night for a murder.

Chapter Ten

Kathi jumped right in with her questions. "What do you think this means, Ryder? Why would Julia get on the phone to Joshua Kincaid the minute we drove away from her house?"

"My first guess would be that the two of them know something about Shawn's death, or at least about what he was mixed up in, though I can't see either of them being responsible for the murder. Of course, as Branson and Arlo always say, appearing innocent is the mark of a successful criminal."

"I wonder how Julia even knows Joshua Kincaid. Do you think that they move in the same social circles?"

"Kincaid said that he and Julia's husband were friends. Of course, Kincaid could have met Julia when she was engaged to Shawn. You and Julia both said that Shawn and Kincaid were close."

"Now that I think about it, I'm sure they would have met. I remember Shawn saying that he'd taken her to a party at Mr. Kincaid's ranch in Kelman."

So Shawn had been to Kelman, and yet he'd never mentioned that when Ryder had talked about the

Burning Pear. Ryder had the feeling he was about to discover things about Shawn that he never expected. "I know Shawn had worked in Kincaid's organization for years. How about you?"

Kathi had to think about that. It seemed forever since she'd worked for the nightclub chain at all. The recent past had so consumed her, kept her so busy just staying alive that her life seemed to be divided into two distinct categories—pre- and post-murder.

"I'd worked at the nightclub in San Antonio for almost a year before I was transferred to Fort Worth, but I didn't know Shawn then, although I had seen him around occasionally when he came to the San Antonio club on business."

Kathi ran her fingers up her neck, fighting the tension that threatened to overwhelm her every time she tried to figure out the maze of events surrounding Shawn's death. "Shawn was hard to figure, ran hot and cold. One day he was friendly, the next standoffish. I always felt things were going on deep inside him. Looking back, it may have been fear. But none of us knew."

Ryder reached across the space between them and laid a hand on her shoulder. "Something will break soon. When it does, the pieces will fall into place."

"I guess. It just seems that it would have been better for everyone if I had just stayed in hiding. You would be home letting Branson and Dillon's high-priced lawyer run things, instead of chasing around the country wondering who might shoot at you next."

"No, you've run for far too long."

She leaned back, letting her head drop to the padded rest on the back of the seat.

Ryder jerked the car into the right lane and sped across the intersection just before the light changed from yellow to red. She fell against him as the front wheel caught the edge of the curb and then fell back to the road with a jarring bump.

"Is this how you get your rodeo excitement fix, now that you're no longer riding broncs?"

"Let's just say that since I was shot at, my suspicion gene has kicked in, big-time." He speeded to the next corner and turned right. A few yards later, he cut back left, down a dark alley. Slowing just a little in the narrow passage between two brick office buildings, he stared into the rearview mirror.

Her anxiety level skyrocketed. "Do you think someone is following us?"

"Probably not, but better safe than sorry. There's a dark blue sedan that's been behind us ever since I hung up the phone after talking to Kincaid. I've noticed him jump from one lane of traffic to another as if he's in a big hurry, but he's never passed us." He peered into the rearview mirror. "If he was following us, I think we've lost him now."

She stared at him, amazed that he'd picked up on everything while she'd been oblivious. "You saw all that behind you?"

"As they say in Texas, my mother didn't raise no fools. You might catch me off guard one night and fire a few bullets into my windshield, but I don't plan to make it nearly that easy to get a second chance at taking me out."

"I could have used you for the past year."

"You could have had me."

His voice had changed in an instant, deepened, taken on a tone that spiked the air between them with a heated rush. It seemed impossible that even with danger twisted all around them, she could have the kind of urges that taunted her now.

During the past year, she'd made herself forget the excitement of walking down the street on his arm, the titillating tingle when she'd curled up next to him in bed, the overwhelming thrill of making love to him. It was part of her survival plan, the strategy that kept her functioning in a world gone mad. In a world where she'd had to abandon her precious baby girl.

She'd convinced herself that one day the killers would be apprehended and she'd walk up to the Randolph ranch and demand custody of Betsy. She'd prepared herself for a fight, but she could have never prepared herself for the reception she'd gotten from Ryder.

She'd remembered him as sexy, cocky, a thrill-a-minute kind of guy. She'd come back to find a brave cowboy who didn't hesitate to take on the men who'd put Shawn in the grave and sent her running for her life.

And he was still the most sexy man she'd ever met.

She turned and looked out the back window. Ryder was driving like a sane man now, evidently convinced that he'd lost the car he'd feared was tailing them. He turned away from the business district and took the up ramp for the Interstate.

"Do we have reservations anywhere?"

"We won't need them. I have the key to a friend's

house. He's out of the country now, but he won't mind if I use his place. I stay there a lot when I'm in the area.''

''Another Arlo?''

''Not even close. K.T.'s a computer nerd, travels all over the world consulting with international banking firms as to how to do their business more efficiently.''

''So how did you two meet?''

''He saved me from failing my first statistics class at the University of Texas. We've been fast buddies ever since, though he never once came out to watch me compete on the circuit. He says he'd be as bored watching me fall from the back of a horse as I'd be watching him punch numbers.''

''Shawn Priest, Arlo, K.T. You have very eclectic tastes in friends.''

''I never really pick my friends. They just kind of happen. Like Shawn. He came out to the rodeo one Sunday afternoon and then came around to meet me. We just hit it off. He started coming out every weekend, driving or sometimes even flying if it was too far to drive. He liked the camaraderie among the rodeo group.''

''I know he talked about you all the time. That's why I came out with him that night to see you perform. I couldn't imagine Shawn that interested in watching men tangle with horses and bulls.''

''I think he envied the freedom I had. He was ready for a change in his life. I never took that to mean escape, though looking back, it must have.''

''I guess tonight we'll find out if Mr. Kincaid knew Shawn felt that way.''

The miles passed, and the downtown district faded away behind them. Ryder tapped his hands on the steering wheel, lost in thought. Finally he turned back to her. "How did you and Shawn connect? You didn't hang out with other people from the club."

"Mostly because I'm a good listener. He started talking about Julia one day, and once he started, he couldn't seem to stop. He was still very much in love with her."

"Shows what I know. I imagined that he was attracted to you the night he brought you with him out to the rodeo grounds."

"No, I think he was playing matchmaker."

"Then he was an even better friend than I thought."

Warmth crept to her cheeks. It would be so easy just to slide into the relationship she'd had before with Ryder. Obviously, he was willing. She wanted the same thing. And yet, she couldn't believe she'd ever live a normal life again.

Ryder laid a hand on her thigh. "We can't seem to solve the mystery with what we know right now, so I say we go to K.T.'s, relax a bit and then follow the glittering neon lights to Kincaid's, the home of Texas ribs and two-steppin'."

"And the best margaritas in Texas," she said, "if you can believe the ads."

"Apparently enough Texans do to make Joshua Kincaid a very rich man. That and a few backroom operations, if you believe my brother Dillon."

"If Joshua does anything illegal in his clubs, he hides it well. I never once saw anything to make me

think the way Dillon does. But then I never suspected
Shawn was involved in anything, either.''

''Trust is not a bad trait, Kathi. Dangerous at
times, but not bad.''

They rode the rest of the way to K.T.'s house in
silence. She wrapped her arms about her chest, fighting a frigid ball that started deep inside her and
swelled until it left her insides quaking from the cold.

Somewhere in Texas, maybe driving down these
same streets in a blue sedan, there was someone who
wanted to kill her for what she didn't know and now
they might kill Ryder, too. But somewhere else, a
family laughed and played with Betsy. She kept that
thought in her mind. It had kept her going for
months. It would have to work for a little while
longer.

RYDER HANDED Kathi her glass of cabernet and then
poured himself a drink from K.T.'s bar. A splash of
bourbon over ice, enough to take the edge off, not
enough to affect his reflexes. He had to be on top of
everything tonight when he talked to Joshua Kincaid.
Had to be aware of every nuance, every blink of the
eye.

Joshua Kincaid and Julia Rodrigue. An unlikely
pair, except that Kincaid had always been known for
having a beautiful woman on his arm. For a man
who'd never been married, he had definitely been
around.

Kathi circled the room, stopping to look at the var-
ious paintings that hung on the walls. ''K.T. has very
good taste. These oils and watercolors are all origi-
nals.''

''He claims he's an expert at finding new artists with talent. He buys them while they're still affordable.''

''Do you see him often?''

''Three or four times a year. Sometimes he comes down to the Burning Pear for a day or two. He's not big on cows, but he loves Mom's cooking. And I stay with him when I'm up this way. As you can tell, he has room to spare.''

''This house is much too large for one person. I'd hate rambling around in it by myself.''

''You haven't seen anything yet. Not only is he big into art, he's a fitness freak. He has one room filled with exercise equipment. He even has a glassed-in extension that houses a pool. It's not large, but it's one of those with an automatic current so that you can actually swim laps in a limited space.''

Ryder finished his drink. He'd expected Branson to return his call by now, but either his brother hadn't gotten his page or he was in the middle of something. Branson would like their meeting with Joshua Kincaid tonight even less than he'd liked their visiting Julia Rodrigue, but Ryder had to do what he felt was right. Still, he wasn't used to conflict between himself and Branson, and the idea of it stretched his raw nerves even tighter.

''I think I'll go for a swim,'' he said. ''Care to join me?''

''I don't have a bathing suit with me.''

''Neither do I.''

She hesitated, and for a minute he thought she was going to take him up on it. But she shook her head and looked away. So different from the Kathi he remembered. Back then, she would have jumped at the chance to go skinny-dipping in a stranger's house, would have been the first one to shed her clothes and dive in.

But that was the Kathi of old. Maybe she was right. Maybe they'd both changed so much over the past few months that they didn't really know each other. Too bad the message hadn't reached his heart.

"I'll take the cell phone with me," he said, "in case Branson calls me back. You can make yourself at home. K.T. would be disappointed if you didn't."

"I will."

He left her standing there, when what he really wanted to do was pick her up, throw her over his shoulder and carry her to the bedroom. But it wasn't what she wanted. Not now, and maybe not ever.

She didn't even turn around when he walked out of the room.

KATHI TRIED watching TV. After five minutes of channel-surfing, she turned it off and dropped the remote to the table at her elbow. She thumbed through a stack of magazines, finally choosing a semi-current edition of *Texas Monthly*. There were articles on everything from politics to religion to a story on branding.

For the rest of Texas, it was business as usual. For her and Ryder, time was running out.

She paced the room and then the hall. The house was quiet, and the silence released all the anxieties that lived in the crevices of her brain. She walked to the back of the house and peered through the glass-and-wood French doors that led to the pool room.

Ryder was swimming naked, and the sight rocked her to her very soul. He was like art in motion, his gorgeous body sliding smoothly beneath the shimmery surface of the pool. The muscles rippled across his strong shoulders as his arms shot out one after the other, rhythmically slicing through the water.

Her lungs constricted, squeezing so tightly, she had to struggle to breathe. Every inch of her was attuned to Ryder, mesmerized by the masculine power of his body as he propelled it against the current. He was everything she didn't need at this moment in her life.

And she had never wanted him more.

Moving as if in a trance, she pushed open the doors and stepped through them. She could stand here, weak and wanting, denying herself the chance to be with the only man she'd ever loved. Or she could step out of her clothes and join him in the water.

There was no mystery about what would happen next. He'd move toward her. Their slick bodies would tangle, their lips would meet. And just for a moment, the fear that ruled her would slip away.

Her heart raced, and a circle of heat rippled through her. Trembling, she fumbled with the buttons on her blouse. Ryder looked up and saw her and then he climbed from the water and started toward her.

The late-afternoon sunlight filtered through the windows, glancing off his body, flickering on the drops of water that clung to the hairs on his chest and his thighs.

She was overcome with desire so real she could

touch it, need so strong she could taste it. The past and the future disappeared. There was only now. Only Ryder.

Only this moment in time.

Chapter Eleven

"Am I dreaming?" Ryder's voice was husky with desire as he took her in his arms.

"I'm not sure."

"If I am, don't you dare pinch me." His lips found hers, and Kathi melted against him. The dampness from his body soaked into her clothes and a raging need took over, so hot she could almost feel the steam rising between them.

He kissed her hard, over and over until she had to pull away to grab a breath. Then she kissed him back, her hands roving his back, her fingers digging into the smooth, naked flesh of his shoulders. Now that she'd let down the barriers, she couldn't get enough of him.

"Some things never change," he whispered. And then his hands took over where hers had left off. He tore her blouse from her body and let it fall to the floor. His mouth was in her hair, at her ear, nibbling and whispering how badly he needed her, all the while loosening the clasp on her bra. The lacy scrap of material fell away, and she reveled in the feel of her nipples pressing against his bare chest.

"Oh, Kathi, I've missed you so much. No matter how I tried to convince myself I didn't."

Liquid heat washed through her as he cradled her breasts in his hands, his thumbs massaging the nipples.

"And I've missed you," she whispered. "Every night and every day." She stretched her fingers and ran them down his abdomen. "I want you, Ryder. All of you. No matter what happens later."

"Good, because I'm not sure I could walk away now and not lose my mind." He slipped his fingers beneath the waistband of her skirt. Finally he worked the button loose and tugged the soft cotton past her hips.

He pulled back and looked at her. "You're even more beautiful than I remember. And softer. Much softer." He trailed his fingers from the center of her breast to her navel and then to the top edge of her panties. He massaged her with his fingers, dipping them beneath the silky fabric, making her moist with desire.

Finally he slid the panties over her hips and she stepped out of them. Ryder was ready. She could see the hardness of him and read the hunger in his eyes. But she couldn't let the moment come and go so quickly, not after she'd waited so long for it. Wiggling, she slipped from his grasp and raced to the water's edge.

She jumped in, sinking until her feet found the bottom. "Aren't you going to join me? You said you wanted to swim."

"You vixen." But he smiled, and her heart nearly stopped beating. The smile transformed him, or maybe it was the fire in his eyes or the teasing tone to his voice. Suddenly he was the Ryder of old.

Sensual, seductive, crazy about her. The thought made her dizzy. The sight of him standing at the edge of the pool like a dark Greek god made her blood sing with desire. The past slipped away.

He came into the water and took her in his arms, his body hard and strong and slick and rubbing against hers. She kissed him and then pulled away. "Are you going to swim or what?"

"The *or what* sounds good to me." He grabbed her and held her close, their bodies slipping and sliding against each other. "I'd love to stay and play," he said, "but it's been too long."

"Much too long," she whispered, wrapping her legs about his hips.

He pulled her onto the length of him. She cried out as he filled her, buried her lips into his shoulder as he thrust inside her. She was sliding over the edge now, soaring with Ryder.

They exploded together. Perfect. The way making love with Ryder had always been. Even now she could feel the beating of his heart against her chest. The fever of passion had broken, but the afterglow still warmed her.

There were a million things she should say, but Ryder would never hear them now. He was fulfilled, mellow, and still inside her.

He touched his lips to hers. "I didn't mean for it be over so quickly."

Over too soon. That must be how it was for him. Intense, his blood surging in a moment of release and then it was done. It was different for her. The passion lasted long after the act. The taste of Ryder stayed on her tongue; the warmth of their lovemaking lingered on her flesh.

A jangling noise broke into her thoughts. Ryder's cell phone.

"I have to get that," he said, looking at her as if he thought an apology was necessary. "It might be Branson."

She nodded, and he climbed out of the pool and grabbed a towel from a basket that rested beneath a potted palm. He dabbed at his face and hair and then knotted the rectangle of thick, white terry around his waist.

She followed him, making a sarong of one towel and using another to dry her dripping hair. She stepped closer to Ryder. She could only hear one side of the conversation, but she could tell he was talking to Branson. He went over every detail of their afternoon.

Well, not *every* detail. Branson didn't need to know how they'd spent the last few minutes. He definitely wouldn't like it.

He was sure she was contaminating his little brother. The problem was, Branson was right. Ryder would figure it out soon. No one needed Kathi Sable and the kind of danger she brought with her.

Ryder held out a hand. She took it and he pulled her into his arms. He was silent now, as if waiting for someone to come on the line. Then he broke into a wide smile.

"Hi, sweetie. Daddy loves you."

Her heart jumped in her chest and then plummeted to her stomach. He was talking to Betsy.

"Say hello to your mama, sweetheart." He stuck the phone to Kathi's ear.

"Da-da, bye-bye. Bally ga-boo."

Kathi opened her mouth, but nothing came out. Her knees gave way and she fell against Ryder as tears burned her eyelids.

She'd heard her Betsy's voice.

RYDER PULLED ON his jeans while Kathi gathered her clothes from the pile where he'd dropped them. He'd followed his instincts, holding the phone to her ear for her to hear their daughter's babbling, a mixture of words and sounds that was distinctly Betsy.

Now he wasn't sure if the move had been a smart one. She had fallen into one of her blue funks, and the moment of passion they'd shared was already no more than a memory. He followed her down the hall to the bedroom, her body still draped in the fluffy towel, her hair wet and plastered to her head.

And still she looked good. He had it bad.

She dropped the clothes onto the bed and then faced him, her stance defiant. "Why did you do that, Ryder?"

He reached for her hand. She jerked it away.

She was overreacting, and he had no feel for what drove her. "Was it so terrible, hearing your daughter's voice?"

"Terrible?" The word was a question and a curse, hurled at him. "No, terrible was handing over the child I'd carried inside me for nine months to a stranger, trusting that person to get my baby to you. Terrible was hoping you would believe she was your daughter and that you'd take care of her."

She was trembling, fighting back tears, and her unhappiness was tearing him apart. Worse, she wouldn't let him hold her, wouldn't let him even try to help. He dug his hands into his pockets and tried to think of something to say that wouldn't anger her more.

"Terrible was the constant ache to hold my baby girl in my arms."

"If I had known why you'd abandoned her, I'd have found you, Kathi. Somehow I would have found you. As it was, I didn't even know she was my child for six months."

"But I knew she was mine." She crumpled to the edge of the bed, her shoulders drooped. "From the first time she stirred inside me, she became part of every breath I took. She was the reason I could keep going, the bit of sunshine in my life. She was my reason for being. She still is."

"Then why was it so painful for you to hear her voice? I mean, I can understand you not wanting to see her because you might lead the danger to her. But I don't understand this." He sat down beside her on the bed. "Betsy's life is filled with love, but none of us can take your place. She needs a mother."

"And I need her, but I can't go through the agony of losing her all over again." Her face twisted in pain.

"You won't have to walk away, Kathi. When this is over, you'll be part of her life."

"Would you agree to my taking her away from the Burning Pear? Would you be able to stand it if she was suddenly ripped out of your life?"

The question stabbed at his heart. He couldn't bear

to think of what his days would be like without
Betsy. He'd miss her hugs in the morning, her laughter when he played ''horsey'' with her, miss tiptoeing
into the nursery at night just to watch her chest rise
and fall in peaceful sleep.

And suddenly he understood what giving up Betsy
had cost Kathi. Tears burned at his own eyes and a
Texas-sized lump formed in his throat. ''No, I
couldn't give up Betsy, not willingly.''

''But I might have to.'' Her voice took on a shaky
timbre. ''There's no guarantee that either we or the
cops will find out who killed Shawn, much less apprehend him. And, as long as danger follows me
around, I can never go near Betsy. Seeing her pictures, hearing her voice—all that does is make it
harder to do what I may be forced to do. If I have
to run again, I'm not sure I'll have the will to go
on.''

''It won't come to that.'' He took her hands in his.
''You're not alone anymore. You have me and the
whole Randolph family to help you. I'll hire guards
if need be.''

''What kind of life would that be for Betsy or for
any of you?''

''A hell of a lot better than living without her
mother.'' He ran his fingers through her hair. The
strands were still damp. The ends curled around his
fingers, the way she had curled around his heart. ''I
can't let you go, Kathi. Betsy needs you. And so do
I.''

She rested her head on his shoulder and let him
hold her close. She didn't promise she'd stay, but
she wasn't talking about leaving. He'd let it go at

that. Besides, if someone didn't find out who killed Shawn Priest, it might be him that had to leave Betsy behind, and by the time he got out of prison, Betsy would be grown.

They sat in the gathering darkness as time slipped away. He wasn't sure who needed whom the most. Tonight he'd have one more chance at finding out the truth. But could he believe anything Joshua Kincaid had to say? Or was the dinner tonight part of a manipulation plot designed by Julia Rodrigue and Kincaid to keep him from learning the truth?

Branson had warned him to keep his eyes and ears open and his back covered. And whatever he did, not to walk into a trap. Especially not one of Joshua Kincaid's making.

KINCAID'S was in full swing when Ryder escorted Kathi through the door. A country song blared from the sound system while four huge screens—one in each corner of the prodigious bar—showed the accompanying video. A cloud of cigarette smoke hugged the ceilings and pulsating lights flickered over a sawdust-covered dance floor.

"Yee-haw," Ryder said, faking a Texas party spirit and an exaggerated drawl. "Now you hang on to my arm, little darlin'. I don't want to have to fight some macho urban cowboy over you."

"Party pooper."

"Who, me?" He held her hand and led her into a fancy turn as they walked past a group of energetic line dancers.

"Don't get too classy," she warned, "or I might

have to fight to keep you. That lady at the bar is already sizing you up."

He tipped his hat in the lady's direction. "I don't know. I think she could take you. Women in black are always good in a catfight."

"In that case, maybe I'll just let her have you and I'll go for the stud in the studs." She nodded toward a man with enough silver on his shirt to open his own mine.

But she was smiling, and he loved the sensation of walking beside her while envious cowboys watched. He liked her eyes when she smiled, her voice when she teased. A blast from the past.

The pleasure was short-lived. He looked up to see Joshua Kincaid hurrying toward them. As usual, the man commanded attention. From the top of his silver-gray hair to the gloss of his expensive western boots, he exuded power. The man was his mom's age, but he walked with the kind of confidence that big bucks and years of experience provided.

Ryder bent his head and put his mouth to Kathi's ear. "Here comes your boss. Let the games begin."

She frowned at him. "He's not the enemy. He'll help us if he can."

He didn't have time to argue with her. Kincaid stopped in front of them, his eyes all for Kathi.

"You look wonderful," he said. "I can't tell you how excited I am that you've moved back to Texas." He took her hand in his and held it a lot longer than was necessary.

"I haven't exactly moved back," Kathi said. "I'm just visiting."

"Nonetheless, it's good to see you here at Kincaid's. I can put you to work tomorrow, if you're looking for a job. Here, or in any of the other cities where we operate.''

''Not just yet,'' she said. ''But I appreciate the offer.''

Finally he turned his attention to Ryder. ''And it's always good to see one of the sons of the prettiest and sweetest woman in all of Texas. I would ask how you've been, but I've been reading about your problems in the paper.'' He clapped Ryder on the back. ''Not that I believe a word of it. Still, I hate to think how Mary must be taking this.''

''Mom's just fine.'' She wasn't, of course, but he detested the way Kincaid always talked as if he and Ryder's mom shared some special friendship. Hated that a man like him sent huge bouquets of flowers on his mother's birthday and gaudy baskets of exotic fruits at Christmas. Kincaid and his dad might have been childhood friends, but that didn't earn him any special closeness with Ryder's mom. Too bad his mother couldn't see that.

Kincaid's gaze roamed the room until he apparently found who or what he was looking for. ''I have to see a man at the bar on some business, but after that, I'll be free for the rest of the evening. Why don't you two go in my office and wait?''

''That's okay. You take your time. We can wait right here.''

''Then have a drink on me,'' Kincaid insisted.

''I'd love a margarita,'' Kathi said.

''The best in Texas,'' Ryder added.

He took Kathi's arm and led her to a table. They'd order a drink and watch Kincaid in action. After all, that was what he was here for. To watch, listen and learn. And try to decide for himself if Joshua Kincaid knew something about Shawn's death.

THE DINING SECTION of Kincaid's was separated from the dance floor and bar area by nothing more than a half wall, allowing the music, voices, laughter and atmosphere to spill over freely. But being the owner, Joshua had no trouble commanding one of the few semiprivate areas. The hostess led them to a small room dominated by a claw-footed oak table.

By the time they'd taken a seat, there were menus in their hands and white cloth napkins in their laps. A minute later, their wineglasses were full.

But Kathi was anything but relaxed. In all the time she'd worked for Joshua Kincaid, she had never dined with him in one of the private dining rooms. Now that she was here, she felt uncomfortable. She couldn't put her finger on why, unless it was knowing how little Ryder and his brothers trusted the man she'd always thought of as unbelievably tough, but fair.

But then their relationship had been strictly that of employee and employer. The barriers between them had been in place, invisible, but invincible. His orders were not to be questioned. His way was the only way. All of his employees knew that and respected it. Or else they weren't employees for very long.

The lines of separation had never bothered her. If anything, they had made her job easier. She was in charge of personnel matters involving the wait staff. Scheduling conflicts were her headache. Hiring and firing decisions were her responsibility unless Mr. Kincaid wanted input.

But the business was his—the profits and the liabilities. That gave him the final say in everything. And to his credit, while he held high standards for his employees, he never expected perfection from anyone but himself. And maybe Shawn Priest, his protégé.

"Did you, Kathi?"

Joshua's question broke into her thoughts. She turned to face him. "I'm sorry. Did I what?"

"I was just saying that I was unaware you and Ryder were friends, and I was wondering if you met him here at my club."

"No, I met him through Shawn."

"Ah, yes." Kincaid toyed with the stem of his wineglass. "Shawn did mention that he had a friend who traveled the rodeo circuit, though I didn't know he was talking about Ryder. Still, I was glad. Shawn needed some new friends." He took his napkin from his lap and touched a corner to his lips.

Ryder leaned in closer. "What was wrong with his old ones?"

Kincaid swirled the wine in his glass, his gaze focused on the crimson liquid. "I don't know if Kathi told you, but Shawn was more than an employee to me. He'd been with me for ten years, more or less grown up under my tutelage. He was smart, picked up on new things as soon as I showed him. And he was ambitious. Two of my favorite qualities in a man."

"But you didn't like his friends."

"No."

Kathi watched Kincaid crumple the white cloth napkin in his fist. The veins in his hands stood out, and his eyes narrowed. "In my mind, they're the reason he's dead."

Kathi trembled at the intensity in Kincaid's voice. She'd never seen him like this before. But if he really believed this, why had he come to them instead of the police? She met his hard gaze. "Who do you think killed Shawn?"

He spread his hands on the table in front of him, the diamond in his ring flirting with the soft light. "I wish I had that answer for you. You don't know how badly I wish I had that answer." He shook his head. "I don't know names or faces."

"Then what do you know?" Ryder asked.

"That Shawn had been hanging out until all hours and then not getting his job done. He showed up late for appointments that had been scheduled for him. Sometimes, especially when the appointment was out of town, he didn't show up at all. I finally told him he'd have to get his act together or hand in his resignation."

"And what was Shawn's response?" Ryder asked.

"He said if that was the way I wanted it, he'd start looking for another job." Sadness crept into Joshua's usually emotionless voice. "It hurt. After all I'd done for him. His attitude hurt. I won't deny that."

For the first time since she'd known him, Kathi felt sorry for Joshua Kincaid. He had more money than he could ever spend, but when it came right down to it, he didn't have the thing that mattered most of all. He had no significant other in his life. Now he didn't even have Shawn.

"I never saw that side of him," Kathi admitted. "I had no idea he wasn't doing his job. It seems as if he would have mentioned it to me or if not, to Ryder."

"Shawn was a master of deception," Joshua said. He reached over and patted her hand comfortingly. "It's just too bad we all found that out too late to help him."

"When did you tell Shawn to find another job?" Ryder's voice was level, his tone unchanged. It was as if none of this had come as a surprise to him. Maybe it was Ryder who knew more than he was telling. Yet he had no reason to keep secrets from her.

Kincaid ran his fingers up and down the stem of his glass, as if he were trying to remember the answer to Ryder's question. Finally he lifted the goblet and drained the rest of the wine.

"It all came to a head around the first of August. That's why I wasn't all that surprised when he just quit coming in. It's the reason I didn't go to the police and report him as missing."

Kathi watched Joshua Kincaid as he talked, trying to determine if he was telling the truth. "Did you know Julia before she married Peyton Ferran?"

"Actually I met Julia through Shawn. But Peyton met Julia at a party on my ranch."

"Was this before or after she broke up with Shawn?"

Kathi didn't miss the sarcasm that had sneaked into Ryder's tone. Neither did Joshua. His face changed in an instant, reverted back to the mask of control and power she was used to seeing on it.

"Julia had come to that particular party with Shawn, but neither I nor Peyton set out to break them up. Shawn managed to do that all by himself. If you don't believe me, ask Julia."

"Why wouldn't I believe you, Mr. Kincaid? After all, you were not only Shawn's friend, but you're a neighbor, just one of the good old boys from Kelman, Texas. One who left the family ranch behind and struck it *filthy* rich in the big city."

"Being successful at what you do is not a crime, Ryder. If it were, the Randolphs would be as guilty as I."

"I never said it was."

"Then I suggest we order dinner," Kincaid said. "Talking about Shawn's murder is hard on all of us, for different reasons, of course. And I've already told you all I know."

"Just one more question," Ryder said. "Do you have any idea as to why whoever killed Shawn decided to bury him on my land?"

"That's the same question the detective who called on me yesterday asked. I didn't have an answer for him, either." Kincaid smiled for the first time since the discussion about Shawn had started. "I suggest the filet for you, Kathi. It's an excellent choice, so tender you can cut it with a fork unless you order it cooked well-done, in which case it will taste like leather. No fault of the meat."

"The filet will be fine," she said. "A small one. I'm not very hungry tonight."

"And for you and me, Ryder, I have a special cut in mind. Man-sized, and fit for a king. It's not on the menu."

"No, I didn't think it would be."

The waiter came and took the orders. A few minutes later, a salad of mixed greens was set in front of them. And when they'd finished the salads, the steaks came out, cooked to perfection. While she picked at hers, both of her dinner companions ate ravenously, as if they didn't have a care in the world.

Texas men and steaks.

Now that was a bond you could count on.

KATHI SAT curled up in the middle of the king-size bed in K.T.'s guest bedroom. Fluffy pillows rested against the headboard and silky sheets wound around her feet. The perfect lover's hideaway. Only, ever since they'd returned from dinner with Mr. Kincaid, Ryder had spent all his time tangling with the mystery that never came any closer to being solved.

He pulled his stocking feet down from the mahogany desk where they'd been resting and dropped them to the carpeted floor. "Okay, I've outlined the inconsistencies in the whole situation."

"That must have taken a pad or two of paper."

"I've condensed them and tried to put them in some sort of time line."

She propped her elbows on her knees. "Did you begin with the actual murder, or with Shawn's telling Joshua Kincaid that he would be looking elsewhere for a job?"

"The murder. Kincaid's claims come in later." He tapped the eraser end of a stubby pencil on the notepad. "I'd like you to listen and give me your first reaction."

"I'll try. The food and the wine—" she glanced

at the clock ''—and the hour have dulled my brain.''
Not to mention the afternoon's lovemaking session.

She had expected Ryder to come home tonight
ready to make love again. She'd wondered how she'd
handle it. It still seemed wrong, could still lead to
heartbreak, and yet, nothing in the past twenty-one
months had seemed as right as making love with Ryder.

But tonight he was consumed by the search for
answers—or at least for the right questions. ''What's
number one on your list?'' she asked.

''You left the scene of the crime and went back
to your apartment. At that point, you weren't aware
that either of the two men had seen you.''

''No, but they could have. I couldn't see their
faces that clearly, only their general movements.''

''But then Kent Quay, the same cop we found
murdered the other night, showed up at your apartment and started asking questions about the murder.''

''Okay, keep going.''

''You told Quay you couldn't identify either of the
men at the scene of the crime and he left. Only he
had some reason to hide the fact that Shawn had been
killed. Or else he turned in the report and someone
else destroyed it. As a result, there was never an investigation into the murder and Shawn's death was
never officially reported.''

''Do you think Quay could have been the man
who called me later and told me to get out of town,
the man who warned me to trust no one, not even
the police?''

''Quite possibly. And you did exactly what he
said. You let the matter drop, but someone still tried

to run you down the very next day right after we'd had lunch. He missed you and hit me, nicking a parked car in the process.''

She stretched her legs and rubbed her temples. ''We've been through all of this before, Ryder. Someone thinks I know who killed Shawn Priest. Someone who's willing to kill me rather than have me talk.''

''Only…if he was so willing to kill you, why didn't he? Why didn't he show up at your house the way Quay did? Why didn't he kill you that night instead of warning you? Besides, it just seems to me that in all the twenty-one months you were on the run, you'd have slipped up a time or two. If someone really wanted you dead, you'd be dead.''

''But someone did try to kill me. The day I met you for lunch to tell you goodbye and then again when I came back to Kelman.''

Ryder walked over and sat down next to her on the bed. ''I don't think they wanted to kill you. They wanted you scared and gone, but not dead. And that's what they got. But you changed all that when you came back to Kelman to see me.'' He dropped his pad of notes to the bed. ''I don't know why, but for some reason the rules have changed. And the reason seems to be connected to me.''

''The drive-by shooter the other night was showing no favoritism. He could have killed either or both of us.'' She shuddered, the cold dread burying itself deep inside her. Ryder wrapped an arm around her and pulled her close. Her head nestled against his strong chest. But even that didn't melt the chill that seeped into the deepest recesses of her heart.

Tonight the terror seemed so imminent, she could hear it blowing with the breeze outside the windows. Out there somewhere in the dark waiting to strike again. Only now it had two targets. Her and Ryder. She'd come back to help him, but her plan had backfired.

She clung to him, and bit back the recriminations that hammered in her mind. She should have never come back to Kelman, Texas. But it was too late to change that.

"Do you always carry a gun, Ryder?"

"No, but I've had one on me since you came back to Kelman. Tonight I have two. I know where K.T. keeps his, and I brought it in here with us. So don't worry. We're well-protected."

"Then I'll sleep soundly tonight."

KATHI WOKE with a start. She opened her eyes and fought to get her bearings. The last thing she remembered was Ryder holding her. She must have fallen asleep in his arms.

She reached across the bed. The covers were rumpled but there was no big, strong cowboy to snuggle against. Ryder must have gotten up during the night. She stretched and untangled her legs from the covers.

"Stay quiet, Kathi."

She caught the scream of alarm in Ryder's whispered warning. She turned to the sound of his voice, barely making out his form in the dark. "What's wrong?"

"Someone's in the house with us. And it's not K.T."

And then she saw the glint of moonlight on the pistol Ryder held in his hands. The terror was no longer imminent. It had arrived.

Chapter Twelve

Adrenaline rushed his veins as Ryder stood with his ear to the closed door. Was this how Branson felt when he had to walk up to a door not knowing what he might find behind it? If it was, his big brother was a very brave man. As for Ryder, life on the suicide circuit seemed a lot more sane and definitely safer than this.

He listened, but all he heard was the sound of his heart pounding in his chest and the air as it was exhaled from Kathi's lungs. She was scared, and he couldn't say anything honest that would make her feel any differently.

The house was silent now, but he'd heard enough to know that someone had opened and closed the front door. And then somebody had tripped over something in the kitchen. He'd heard the clatter. Only he had no idea how many people had crept into the house in the few seconds the door had been open.

And not knowing left him and Kathi extremely vulnerable. "I want you to lock yourself in the guest bathroom, Kathi. And I want you to take this with you." He walked over to the bed and handed her

K.T.'s pistol. He couldn't help but notice that her hands were as cold as ice when she took it. "It's loaded, so be careful. If anyone besides me comes to the door, use it."

"What if it's only a friend of K.T.'s? He lets you come here when you want to. Maybe he shares his home with other friends, as well."

"If that's the case, I'll be the one at the bathroom door. Now get inside and don't come out. No matter what you hear, don't come out."

"Where are you going?"

"To find out who's out there."

"No, you can't go." She grabbed hold of his arm. "Call 911. Let the police handle this."

"By the time the police drive out here, we'll be dead."

She let go of his arm. He kissed her quickly and walked away before he lost his own nerve and couldn't leave her. When he looked back, she was only a dark form, outlined by the bit of moonlight that filtered through the curtains, but his mind pictured her the way he knew she looked. Frightened, but with her chin jutted out to convince herself she was up to this.

He waited for the brush of wood on wood as the bathroom door closed before he stepped into the narrow hallway. There was no moonlight here. Just blackness. He kept his back to the wall as he crept toward the kitchen. Then he saw it—a circle of light that came from under the door of K.T.'s bedroom.

His pulse quickened. If the man who'd entered the house had any business being here, he'd have flicked on an overhead light. He'd never stumble around in the dark, relying on a flashlight to find his way around.

The man in the next room was here to kill him and Kathi. The knowledge lodged in his throat, like a huge pill that was too big to swallow. A second later it plunged straight to his gut. The fear was gone now, replaced by an anger so intense he could barely keep from just barging through the door and pulling the trigger over and over until the man was as dead as Shawn Priest was. As dead as he and Kathi would be if he didn't end this now.

Holding the gun steady, his finger on the trigger, he kicked K.T.'s bedroom door open and stepped aside. Something hard crashed into his arm and then rammed into his knees. Curses burst from his mouth as his knees buckled under him and the pistol flew from his hand and skidded away.

THE PISTOL FELT ponderous in Kathi's hand, as if it might be hard to control. She paced the small bathroom. Six steps to the back wall and six steps back to the front. On one of them, her foot landed on the tuft of plush terry that served as a bath mat. A strange thing to notice when her mind was whirling dizzily.

She'd followed Ryder's orders. Now she wondered why. He wasn't a cop. He was brave, and protective, and a man, but he was no more trained in apprehending killers than she was. Yet, she was locked away in a bathroom and he was roaming through a dark house alone, searching for a man who might have followed them home with the intent to kill.

But then the quiet was broken. Loud voices.

Curses. Ryder's and someone else's. A voice she didn't recognize. Something slammed against the wall.

She had to do more than stay locked away. She steadied the gun and opened the bathroom door. Once she reached the hall, she pinpointed the source of the noise. Her heart was racing, her stomach a rumble of nerves, as she stopped at the open door to K.T.'s bedroom. All she could see were two dark forms, struggling in the shadows.

"Stop or I'll shoot," she said, the second she made out which form was Ryder.

The trespasser stopped. For one second. And then he bounded through the open window. She tossed Ryder the pistol, and he took off after the man. She doubted he'd catch him. He was limping, so evidently the man had landed a blow to Ryder's injured knee.

She leaned against the wall until she caught her breath. Now there was nothing to do but wait, and pray that Ryder walked back through the door. She didn't care if he caught the other man—not now. All she wanted was Ryder alive. She went to the phone and dialed 911.

RYDER STOOD on K.T.'s lawn in the predawn grayness, watching the police car pull away. They'd come out in response to Kathi's call, but their trip had been wasted. The man had gotten away. Still, they'd taken prints and they had the gun the man had left behind. At this point Ryder had little faith they'd turn up anything. Dead ends were getting to be a habit in this case. There was no reason to expect anything different this time.

He put an arm around Kathi's waist. "I was so close to having him. He must have heard me in the hall."

"I'm just glad you're okay. I'm surprised he didn't shoot you after he slammed the weight-lifting pole into your legs."

"He would have, if I hadn't managed to grab his arm and pull him down with me. I wrestled the gun from his hand and threw it. Don't ask me how. It all happened so fast."

"But you don't have a clue who it was?"

"No. It wasn't anyone I've met before. It was dark, but not so dark I wouldn't have recognized someone I knew."

"Why do you think he was in K.T.'s room?"

"He was working his way down the hall. If we'd been fast asleep, and he'd taken us by surprise as I'm sure he intended to do—"

"I know, but don't say it."

She fitted herself into the crook of his arm. He pulled her closer and rested his chin in the silky hair on the top of her head.

"But he was just an ordinary man," she said. "For nearly two years, he's held me captive though he's never laid a hand on me. He not only stole my life, he robbed me of the first year of my baby's life. He has me jumping at every shadow, afraid to close my eyes at night. And he's just an ordinary man with two eyes, two arms, two legs."

"He isn't a man the way I measure a man. He's

a snake, a belly-crawler, something to be ground under a real man's feet.''

''So now we have no one left to go to for answers except Bull Ruffkins's brother. Do you really think that seeing him will get us anywhere?''

''We can't give up now. We'll drive to his place in the morning. He's expecting us. After that, we'll catch a flight and be back in Kelman by dark. It will be a busy day, so I say we go back to bed and try to get some sleep.''

His legs throbbed from the attack, and his body ached from the fight. He wasn't used to being thrown around since he'd left the rodeo circuit. ''You were great tonight,'' he said, leading her back into the house.

Kathi squeezed his hand. ''We did make a pretty good team.''

''We always did.''

They had been good together tonight, and they had been fantastic this afternoon at the pool. Damn. He should be tired. He should want sleep. But the urges running through his blood had nothing to do with sleep. ''Race you to the bedroom?''

''You're on, but you'd never be able to catch me tonight.''

But he only let her get a couple of steps ahead before he swooped her up in his arms and carried her the rest of the way.

KATHI LAY awake after they'd made love, and listened to the steady, reassuring sounds of Ryder's breathing. It was hard to believe that it had been less than two weeks since she'd picked up the newspaper in Mobile, Alabama, and read that Ryder was being questioned in connection with Shawn's murder.

Hard to believe that she was here with him, still warm and moist from their lovemaking, the way she'd been so many times in her dreams. So much had happened since they'd first met at the rodeo grounds in Fort Worth. Yet she remembered the night as if it were yesterday.

Ryder had swaggered up to them after his event and flashed his boyish smile, the one that was forever burned into her memory. He'd smelled of horseflesh and leather and seemed to reek of testosterone. To say she'd developed a killing case of lust at first sight would be an understatement.

For two weeks, she'd been happier than she'd ever been before. Two weeks and then her whole life had changed. She'd left her job, her house, and she'd left Ryder. A month later, alone and running for her life, she'd found out she was pregnant. And from that moment on, keeping her unborn baby alive and healthy had become her life.

And finally her daughter had come screaming and pushing into the world. Healthy. Perfect. Kathi's arms began to ache, the way they always did when she thought of her baby. She folded them across her chest. And still they ached.

She stared at the shadows that stalked the ceiling. Her mood changed in an instant, and she shuddered as if the temperature had suddenly dropped below freezing. She burrowed beneath the covers and snuggled next to Ryder, but the warmth could not penetrate to the chill that filled her heart.

The sense of danger loomed inside her, even

stronger than it had tonight when they'd faced the killer. Maybe it was a typical response, a delayed reaction to fear.

But that's not the way it seemed. She touched Ryder's shoulder and shook him until he woke. He rolled over, instantly alert.

"What's wrong?"

"Call your house. Please call your house and ask about Betsy."

He held her close. "Betsy will be sleeping and so will everyone else." He wrapped an arm about her. "We'll call as soon as the sun comes up, but Betsy's fine. If she wasn't, Branson would let us know."

She knew he was right. If anything was wrong, Branson would have called them. Ryder held her until the trembling stopped, but the chill still clung to her heart, like icicles that refused to melt. And she knew she wouldn't be satisfied until Ryder made the call.

BRANSON STOOD in the warm kitchen at the Burning Pear, speaking to Lacy in hushed tones. He'd just gotten off the phone from talking with Ryder, and a hard rage was weakening his self-control. "Ryder damn well better come back here and let the professionals handle this investigation before he gets himself killed." He bit back the rest of what he felt. Lacy didn't deserve his tirade. Ryder did.

Lacy laid a hand on his arm. "Ryder's a grown man, Branson, the same as you are. I know you and your brothers think of him as your little brother, but he's twenty-six and a father."

"Then it's time he started acting like it. He's not trained in law enforcement."

"Neither was Langley when he took over as acting sheriff while we were on our honeymoon. You trusted him, and he did a bang-up job."

"Langley's different. He'd had experience. He listened to what Arlo and other knowledgeable guys told him and didn't go off half-cocked the way Ryder has. I've offered to go with him to talk to these people he's determined to question, but he won't hear of it. He insists that he can get more out of them if he goes as Shawn's friend and not accompanied by a cop."

"That sounds reasonable to me."

"It doesn't to me, and after last night, you'd think he'd be begging me to come up there with him or else he'd just pack up and come home. It's a miracle he's alive."

"But he is alive. And from what you said, he handled himself just fine. Kathi did, too." Lacy eased into his arms. "Ryder's a Randolph, Branson. He's got the same blood running through his veins as you and Langley and Dillon. He's not doing a bit more than any of you would be doing if the woman you loved was in danger."

"Hmmph."

"What's that grunt supposed to mean?"

"All we know about Kathi Sable is that she gave birth to Betsy. She might not be the innocent witness she claims to be. She could be involved in this up to her pretty little neck."

"If that's the way you talk to Ryder, I'm not surprised he's not listening to you."

"All I know is that if anything happens to Ryder, Mom will be devastated."

"We all will, Branson. But that doesn't mean we can run his life for him."

She rose up on tiptoe and kissed him, and he held her close. "How did I ever find someone like you?"

"You were lucky. Very lucky. And don't forget it."

He looked up at the sound of his mother's footsteps coming down the hallway. "Okay, My Smart and Beautiful Wife, what do I tell Mom about all of this? The first thing she'll want to know is, have I heard from Ryder."

"Tell her the truth. The whole truth, about everything. The secrets have gone on too long around this house. Besides, she can handle it, and she has a right to know."

"I have a right to know what?" Mary Randolph stood in the door staring at them. "Has something happened to Ryder?"

Branson met her gaze and wondered when her hair had turned from blond to silver, when her back had stooped a little, when she'd gotten the wrinkles that lined her eyes. But Lacy was right. His mom was tough, probably the toughest of them all.

She stood quietly, waiting for his answer.

"Ryder's okay," he assured her. "Bullheaded, but okay. Sit down and I'll tell you all about it."

Betsy's yells drifted down the hallway. Branson glanced at the kitchen clock. Six a.m. Right on schedule.

"I'll get her," Lacy said. "You two talk." She

laid a hand on his mom's shoulder as she walked past her.

Branson watched the soft sway of his wife's hips as she went to rescue Betsy from the crib. Lacy was right. He was a very lucky man.

CYRUS RUFFKINS poked around his tractor-repair shop, too agitated to work and with too much to do to sit and wait for Ryder Randolph and Kathi Sable to show up. He rubbed his hands on his grease-stained overalls and stepped around a box of crank-case oil.

He hoped his brother wasn't in trouble, but he wouldn't have a clue if he was. Bull had moved up in the world and left his family behind. Cyrus hadn't heard from him in over a year.

Bull wore designer shirts and carried a wad of money around in a silver money clip. He paid forty dollars for a haircut. He'd told Cyrus that once. Hell, Cyrus could buy a week's groceries for little more than that, and his seven-fifty haircut suited him just fine. He reached up and ran his fingers along the stubble that poked outside his collar.

Still, if Bull was in some kind of trouble, he'd like to know about it. Families should stick together, even if one of the members thought he was too good for the others.

Cyrus heard the car drive into the driveway. He peeked out the window. He liked what he saw and relaxed a little. Ryder Randolph wasn't one of those fancy city guys. He wore a Stetson that had seen its share of sun and rain. His boots had a little wear on them, too. And Kathi Sable looked down-to-earth, as well. Pretty, but she wasn't weighed down by a lot of paint on her face.

He walked over and opened the door.

KATHI SAT on the edge of a swivel chair that Cyrus Ruffkins had rolled away from a cluttered desk. She'd tried to stay optimistic, but by the time the introductions were finished, the sinking feeling had already settled inside her. The man seemed too genuine, too naive to know about the kind of cold-blooded murder she'd witnessed. Bull might know, but not Cyrus.

"We've been trying to locate your brother," Ryder said. "We were hoping you could help us with that."

"Did you try his town house?"

"We tried the phone number you gave us. The landlady said he'd moved about six months ago and left no forwarding address."

"That sounds just like Bull. Moving off without even telling me. After all, I'm just his brother."

"Who does he work for?" Kathi asked.

"For himself. Has for as long as I can remember. Every time he worked for someone else, he got fired."

"Why is that?" Ryder asked.

"He's got a smart mouth on him, and he hates taking orders."

Ryder propped his foot on a strange-looking contraption that probably fit into the tractor whose parts were scattered about the shop. "What kind of work does he do?"

"You don't know?"

"I wouldn't be asking if I did."

Cyrus rubbed his stained and beat-up fingers across his chin. "He's a bookie. Football, baseball, basketball, wrestling. You take the odds, he takes the cash."

"That's illegal."

"Right, and dangerous. But that's not the kind of thing that bothers Bull. He likes fast money. And he don't cotton to hard work. Take this place." Cyrus spread his hand and motioned to include the whole shop. "It's been in the family for years. I went to work here right after high school and then took over the operations entirely when my dad died. But do you think Bull would ever get his hands dirty?"

"I guess not." Ryder picked up a wrench and turned it over in his hands. "Did you ever hear Bull talk about a man named Shawn Priest?"

"Shawn Priest." Cyrus repeated the name and nodded his head. "Was that the young man who worked for Kincaid's nightclub?"

Kathi's interest piqued. "That's the one. Did Bull talk about him much?"

"Bull doesn't talk about anyone much except himself, but Shawn did come by the shop with him one day. Bull had some old black Chevy that was giving him problems. That's when you see my brother, when he needs you."

"Do you remember when that was?" Ryder asked.

"I'd say around two years ago, give or take a few months. All the car needed was a tune-up, but Bull never was good at fixing anything."

"Did Shawn mention being in any kind of trouble?"

"No, he probably didn't say two words the whole time they were here. He just stood around with Bull while I did all the work. It wasn't one of the fancy cars Bull usually drives, though, and that Priest fellow didn't talk like it belonged to him. I don't know, maybe Bull was getting it fixed for a friend who was short on cash. He isn't all bad."

"And that was the only time you met Shawn?" Ryder asked.

"That was it."

"What kind of car was it that Bull had you work on?"

"A black Chevy, about five years old."

"Then Bull never mentioned anything about Shawn being in some kind of trouble?" Kathi stared at Cyrus, almost willing him to remember something, but he shook his head and scratched his chin. "Naw. Not to me."

Kathi barely listened to the rest of the discussion. A clock rang out nine chimes, melodic, out of place in the clutter of the machine shop.

"Do you like the chimes?" Cyrus asked.

"They're very pretty," Kathi answered.

"Bull brought that for Momma back before she died. She loved it, always loved anything Bull brought her. Probably cause he didn't buy her much. When she died, I hung the clock down here. It always surprises people when it chimes."

"It is unique," she agreed. But she was anxious to get out of the repair shop. Anxious to get out of Fort Worth.

Finally Ryder gave up. Cyrus walked to the door with them. "I hope Bull's not in some kind of trouble. You'll let me know if he is, won't you? I'm here most every day, 'cept Sunday, but I'm going on vacation starting Monday. The place will be closed down until I get back.''

"We'll let you know.''

Kathi followed Ryder back to the truck. "Nothing again,'' she complained.

"I wouldn't say that. It was a black Chevy that plowed into me in Fort Worth the day after Shawn was killed.''

"Then it could have been Bull driving that car. That might have been the car Cyrus repaired.'' Excitement stirred and swelled inside her. "This could be our first real lead.''

"Only no one knows how to find Bull Ruffkins.''

She let the new information mingle with the little she already knew. "Do you think he was the man who broke into K.T.'s house last night?''

"It's definitely possible.''

"What do we do now?''

"Go back to Kelman. I'd like to discuss this with Branson and Arlo while we wait to hear from the Fort Worth police on the gun and fingerprints left at K.T.'s.''

"Back to Kelman, dragging the danger behind us? Even if Bull is the man we're looking for, he could be anywhere. And he may not be working alone. There were *two* men at Shawn's murder scene.'' She yanked her seat belt tight. "*You* go back, Ryder. Let your brothers help you clear yourself of any charges the D.A. may be cooking up against you. You belong in Kelman. I don't, and I have nothing but danger to offer.''

He threw on the brake and brought the car to a screeching halt. "Do you really think I would just let you leave on your own? What kind of man do you think I am?"

"It's not just you, Ryder. It's your family we have to think about. It's Betsy."

"The answer is *no*. I don't want you out of my sight until this is all over. If you leave I'll only follow you."

"And what if you're arrested?"

"Then you can stay at Arlo's if you insist, or you can go to the Burning Pear. My brothers will see that you're protected."

"Nothing would make your brother Branson happier than if I just disappeared into thin air."

"The way you did two years ago." His muscles bunched into tight knots. "When this is over, when you're safe and the killer is behind bars, then you can walk, if that's the way you want it. But I am not throwing you to the hungry wolves. If we get eaten, we get eaten together."

She didn't argue. It would be no use. She closed her eyes and tried to picture Betsy the way she'd looked in the photographs, smiling, clapping her hands. But the image faded, and it was Shawn's lifeless body she say, falling to the hard concrete.

THE CELL PHONE RANG. Ryder answered. He expected it to be Branson but it was Dillon who said hello.

"I need you to be back in Kelman by seven o'clock tonight."

"What's up?"

"I've heard rumblings that your arrest is imminent."

"What's changed?"

"The rumor is that the rangers now have a motive to go along with the fact that Shawn's body was found on our property."

"What is it?"

"A love triangle. You, Kathi and Shawn Priest. He was in love with her. You stole her away. She threatened to go back to Shawn, and you killed him."

"Your rumors come with lots of details."

"And that's the condensed version." Dillon paused to tell Petey not to push his toy race car across the antique buffet. "At any rate, the lawyer I've been talking to in Seattle has agreed to come down here and take your case. He's flying in this afternoon and wants to meet with us tonight."

"We should be there. But I picked up a very interesting bit of information from Cyrus Ruffkins."

"Really? What is it?"

Branson told him about the car, and he could hear a little more optimism in Dillon's tone when he spoke again.

"You've done a great job of investigating, but it's time to turn this over to the police."

"I agree."

"And, Ryder, Branson told me about what happened last night. It sounds like you and Kathi handled things real well. It's damn good to hear your voice after that."

"Who else did Branson tell?"

"All of us."

"Mom included?"

"It seemed best. She always knows when something is wrong anyway, and if we don't tell her the truth, she thinks the worst."

Ryder felt the sharp edge of regret slice into his determination. "Did she take it okay?"

"She's trying to. She has Betsy to take care of, and that at least keeps her busy. She can't just sit and worry. What about Kathi?"

"She's threatening to run again. I'm not about to let her."

"If you did, you'd never forgive yourself. I don't know what she is to you, but she's your daughter's mom. And take it from a man who learned the hard way. Family's everything."

"Speaking of family, Mom's not leaving the ranch alone, is she?"

"Never. I've told her that Langley, Branson or myself is to go with her anytime she needs something from town. Even Ashley, Lacy and Danielle are staying at the ranch unless they have one of us for an escort. We're taking no chances."

"I'm sorry to do this to all of you."

"You didn't. And maybe it'll be over soon."

A beeping noise interrupted their conversation. "It looks like I have another call coming in," Ryder said. "But unless something big happens, I'll be there tonight. We have a late-afternoon flight out of Fort Worth."

"I'll see you then. And, little brother, be careful."

"Always."

Ryder punched the button on the phone and took

the next call. "Ryder Randolph. What can I do for you?"

"Ryder." The voice was feminine, little more than a whisper.

"Who is this?" he asked.

"It's Julia Ferran. I need to talk to you and Kathi."

He looked up to find Kathi studying his responses. He mouthed the word *Julia* so that she'd know who he was talking to. "Did you think of something else?" he asked.

"Yes. I think it could be important."

"Kathi and I are on our way to the airport to catch a flight home, but if it's important, we can make a quick stop at your place."

"It's important, but I'd rather you didn't come here. Peyton was upset that I talked to you yesterday, and I wouldn't want him to know that I'm seeing you again. There's a park a couple of miles from my house. We could meet there."

A park. That sounded too much like a trap. "How about the parking lot of a supermarket? I like the idea of people around."

"A parking lot would be fine. But if I'm late, don't call my house, and whatever you do, don't leave a message on my answering machine."

She gave him directions to an area just off the Interstate, one he would be able to find without difficulty. He pushed the rental car a few miles over the speed limit. He couldn't wait to hear what Julia had to share with them that was worth risking the ire of her husband.

JULIA OPENED her car door and climbed out. She looked around nervously and then crossed the few yards to where they sat waiting. Kathi thought she looked much paler in the bright sunshine than she had in the dimly lit house.

Ryder got out from behind the wheel of the rental car and opened the back door. "Get in," he said. "This will be better than going inside or standing in the wind."

She hesitated, and Kathi could have sworn it was fear she saw reflected in Julia's deep green eyes. But Julia crawled into the back seat and scooted to the middle. And that's when Kathi noticed the purple smudges of a makeup-covered bruise on her right cheek.

Julia glanced out the back window and then wound her hands into fists.

Kathi scooted around in the seat so that she faced Julia. "Is something wrong? You look upset."

She shook her head unconvincingly. "I've just been thinking about Shawn and how he was shot down like a dog in the street." Her voice broke on the words. "And I remembered something that might help you find his killer."

"We appreciate that," Ryder said. His voice was even and reassuring, though Kathi was sure the calm was forced. "Tell us anything that comes to mind."

She exhaled sharply, as if beginning would be the toughest part. "It was in the winter, not last year, but the year before. Peyton and I had flown to the Cayman Islands. He has property down there, an investment in a resort. He likes to fly down every so often and meet with the other investors.'' She paused.

''The islands are a popular vacation spot,'' Ryder said, ''a real beach-lover's paradise.''

But Kathi was thinking more along the lines of a rich man's paradise, for those who kept their fortunes in banks outside the U.S. Kathi couldn't help but wonder if Julia's husband hadn't stashed a bit of cash down there.

Julia clasped and unclasped her hands. ''We had gotten off the plane and were hurrying toward the baggage check when I almost ran into Shawn and his friend Bull. I mean we were closer than I am to the two of you right now. The leather valise Shawn was carrying brushed the fabric of my skirt.''

''I'm surprised,'' Kathi said. ''Every time Shawn took a vacation in the winter, it was to fly to Joshua Kincaid's ski condo in Colorado. Did he say why he was in the Cayman Islands?''

''That's just it. He didn't say anything. I don't think he even saw me at first. He and Bull were both looking straight ahead and walking fast. I called to him, but he didn't turn around.''

''That's strange,'' Ryder said. ''Are you sure it was him?''

''I'm sure. When you've slept with a man for months, when you've been in love with him, you don't mistake him when he practically runs into you.''

''Then why do you think he didn't speak to you?'' Ryder asked. ''Had your breakup been that bitter?''

''No, he'd been hurt and angry at first, but we'd

talked since then. He seemed to understand that I needed more security than he could offer.''

Security or money? Kathi had her own ideas on that subject. Shawn hadn't been poor, but he definitely wasn't in Peyton Ferran's league. ''Did Peyton think it was Shawn that you saw?''

''No.'' Her voice dropped to a whisper and she lowered her gaze to the hands that still twisted in her lap. ''At least he said he didn't. He held my arm when I tried to run after Shawn, and told me I was mistaken. It didn't seem worth arguing about at the time, but now, after what happened to Shawn, I wonder if it was important.''

''It could be,'' Ryder said. ''Did you know Bull Ruffkins well?''

She scowled. ''Enough not to like him. He's a smart aleck, and when Shawn was around him, he tended to pick up his arrogant habits. He was probably the main contributor to our breaking up, besides Shawn himself.''

She turned her head, peering out each of the side windows and then looking out the back of the car. ''I have to go now. Peyton sometimes comes home during the day, and he'll wonder where I am.''

The more Julia said about Peyton, the less Kathi liked him, and she'd never even met the man.

Ryder laid a hand on Julia's. ''Was there trouble between Shawn and your husband?''

Bingo. Ryder was on target. Fear flickered in Julia's eyes, and her body went rigid. ''I have to go,'' she said. ''I've told you all I know. Don't call me again. Please don't call me again.''

She turned and bolted from the car, her feet flying

as she sped across the few yards of cement to her Mercedes. She jumped into it and drove off without a glance in their direction.

"Do you think it was Shawn she saw in the Cayman Islands?" Kathi asked as Ryder turned the key in the ignition and pulled out of his parking spot.

"Yep." He nudged his hat back, and for the first time that day, a grin split his lips. "But she was lying about Peyton and Shawn's relationship. I think I'll see what Branson or Arlo can dig up about Peyton Ferran's background."

"I have a feeling he's not a good man to cross," she said, remembering the fear in Julia's eyes and the bruise on her cheek.

"I have that same feeling. And Shawn was not the kind of guy to take someone stealing his girl without putting up a fight."

Kathi stared out the window as Ryder headed the car toward the airport. Peyton Ferran was rich, influential and mean enough to frighten his own wife. But was he the kind of man who'd kill and then do whatever he had to do to make sure he was never caught?

But if either Bull or Peyton Ferran killed Shawn, why did they bury the body on the Burning Pear? The questions boggled the mind. And now Ryder was about to be arrested for a murder she knew he didn't commit.

Chapter Thirteen

They had landed in San Antonio, picked up his truck with the new windshield and were driving toward Kelman by the time Ryder's phone rang again. This time it was Branson, and he could tell by the greeting something was terribly wrong.

"What now?" he asked, his hand tightening around the phone.

"You need to get back to the ranch as quickly as you can. A warrant has been issued for your arrest."

Ryder heard the words, but couldn't quite believe them. He'd thought he'd prepared himself for this possibility, but evidently he hadn't. Maybe a man like him couldn't prepare himself to be locked behind bars.

He tugged his hat low on his head. "When did this happen?"

"The ranger who questioned you the other day just called me. He said it would be better if you came in voluntarily. I agree with him."

"So where do I turn myself in?"

"In Kelman. At my office. How's that for irony? Once you turn yourself in, they'll lock you up in

Eagle Pass. But you can come to the Burning Pear first. Dillon, Langley and I would all like to walk in with you.''

His brothers. There had never been a time in his life when they hadn't been there for him. The Randolphs, all together. ''I'd like that.''

''This is only temporary, Ryder. You know that. Dillon says they don't have a case and that they know a jury would listen to what Kathi has to say. She's a credible witness.''

''I guess we'll find out if it's temporary.'' Ryder beat a fist against the steering wheel. ''Did you hear who testified that there was a love triangle?''

''Not officially, but I know Peyton Ferran has talked to the investigator.''

Ryder was not the least bit surprised. ''I'll need someone to look after Kathi, Branson. I can't leave her unprotected.''

''There's always Arlo.''

''Does that mean you don't want the job?'' Ryder waited. Branson had always been the Doubting Thomas of the family, but he'd never known him not to be fair.

''We'll do it any way you want it, Ryder. I know you'd do the same for me, if it ever came to that.''

''Thanks.''

Ryder finished the conversation quickly and turned to Kathi. ''There's a warrant out for my arrest. I'm going to turn myself in.''

''This is all my fault.'' Her lips quivered, and moisture glistened in her eyes.

That was the last thing he'd been prepared for. He slowed the truck and drove onto the shoulder. When he'd come to a complete stop he pulled her into his arms.

"We've already talked about this. You didn't kill anyone. This is not your fault."

"I ran. I saw Shawn murdered and I ran."

"You didn't just run. You reported the murder to the police. And if you hadn't run, you'd be just as dead as Shawn. What would that have solved?"

"I don't know, but I dragged you into a fight that was never yours."

"And it was never yours, either, Kathi. The only thing both of us did was befriend Shawn Priest. That's all. Besides, it wasn't your doing that Shawn was buried on Randolph land."

"No matter what you say, Ryder, no one was trying to kill you until I walked back in your life. I never should have run, or I should have kept running."

He rocked her to his chest. "You should be here. You have a daughter who needs you. Let me take you to her, Kathi. Let me take you to the Burning Pear. Do this for me."

She stiffened. "No. Please, Ryder, I'll do anything you ask except that. I will not lead the killer to Betsy. Not even if I never get to see her again."

"Okay, baby, okay." He buried his mouth in her hair. It smelled of wildflowers and springtime. The fact struck him like a thunderbolt. He wouldn't lie beside her tonight, and maybe not for many nights to come. "I'll miss you," he said, already feeling the pain of separation.

"Surely you won't be in jail long. Someone will have to listen to reason."

"I hope it's you. If you won't go to the Burning Pear, then you can stay at Arlo's. But promise me one thing."

"If I can."

"Promise me you won't run away again."

"I promise to stay and testify that you're innocent." She lifted her face to his. Her lips parted, and he met them. Desire hit him like a jolt of electricity, and he was amazed that even with his world falling apart, he wanted her so desperately. Or maybe it was *because* his world was falling apart.

He pulled away from her and started the truck. A mile down the road, he gave in to the hunger, knowing it might be a long, long time before he got to satisfy it again.

He turned down a dirt road.

"Where are we going?"

"Somewhere we can be alone."

RYDER FOUND a spot under the splotchy shade of a persimmon tree. He didn't have a blanket, but the grass grew low and thick here, and there was no one around to interfere. He dropped to the grass and toed off his boots.

Kathi looked past him, to a scattering of wildflowers that dotted the grassland, bluebonnets and larkspur and some bright red Indian paintbrush. He reached up, grabbed her hand and pulled her down beside him. "Ever made love with a jailbird?"

"Oh, Ryder, don't joke about this. It's too serious."

"That's why we have to joke." He feathered her lips with quick kisses, and her body temperature climbed. "I'm not worried about me," he said, tangling his fingers in her hair. "I'm innocent and I'll get off. I just hate that I have to leave you."

"I'll be fine. I'm sure Arlo is a very competent bodyguard."

"Maybe, but he can't take care of all your other needs like I can."

No. No man ever had. From the first night they'd been together, there had never been anyone for her but Ryder. Her inhibitions melted as the kiss deepened. She parted her lips, and he took possession of her mouth, coaxing, thrusting, thrilling.

"Undress me, Ryder," she said. "I want the feel of your fingers all over me. Undress me nice and slow, and then I'll do the same for you."

"Slow. Are you into torture?"

"Yes, delicious, erotic, sensual torture. I want your hands to find all the parts of me that go crazy when you touch me. I want this day to be remembered for something good, and not everything bad."

"I think I can handle that." A lazy, devastating smile split his lips, as if they had all the time in the world, as if he wasn't about to be arrested.

But she couldn't think about that now. Couldn't spoil the little time they had left together. Lying back on the grassy carpet, she closed her eyes as his fingers started working on the buttons of her blouse.

When the last one fell open, he slipped the blouse from her shoulders and down her arms. The wind feathered her flesh, and Ryder's lips brought her to life. He kissed her shoulders, the base of her neck, the line of cleavage. She writhed in pleasure.

"You're beautiful in the sunlight," he whispered,

nibbling at her earlobe. "I like the way your skin glistens, and the way your hair turns the color of wheat when the light hits it."

"Then let's always make love in the afternoon."

"Let's just always make love."

"Always."

They both played the game, pretending there would be an always, pretending that he wasn't about to go to jail for a murder he didn't commit while the real killer still walked the street. The time they had now had to be savored and cherished. Remembered and dreamed about.

He loosened the clasp on her bra, and her breasts fell free. He tasted first one and then the other, his tongue circling the nipples until they stood straight up, begging for more. And then he pushed up her skirt. His fingers found the smooth flesh of her inner thighs, circling, riding, until his thumbs brushed against her panties. She was going crazy with wanting him, and yet she didn't want him to finish. Didn't want the lovemaking to end.

He slipped his fingers underneath the waist of her panties and tugged. He slipped them down her legs and over her feet. And then he went to work with his tongue, pushing back her skirt and finding all the places that sent her rocketing out of her mind.

Her insides erupted in a flow of hot liquid. She sucked in the pleasure and then rolled to her side. "Now it's your turn, cowboy."

"If it gets any better, I may not live through it." He lay on his back, pulling down his hat to shade his eyes from the setting sun. Only his smile still showed.

"It's going to get lots better," she whispered, already tugging loose the snaps on his western shirt. When it fell open, she tangled her fingers in the spray of dark hairs. She roamed his chest with her mouth, teasing with quick kisses and nibbles. When she reached his waist, she unbuckled his belt and unsnapped his jeans.

She eased them over his hips, giving him the same slow, brushing strokes he'd given her. She kissed him, stroked him, until he writhed in pleasure.

"Climb on top of me," he said. "I want to be inside you."

She straddled him, moving in slow, steady strokes while he thrust deep inside her. Over and over until neither of them could hold back the passion that was driving them wild.

They exploded together, in the fading sunshine, on a day neither of them would ever forget.

"I love you," she whispered.

"Even though we've changed?"

"All the more because we've changed."

"And I love you," he whispered. "Because some things never change."

THE MAN in the brown hat stood outside Gus's Corner Café, picking at his teeth. The smell of onions was strong on his breath, but he didn't care. He wasn't in Kelman to make friends.

He was here to take care of business.

Kathi Sable had cost him his job. Worse, he was the one who'd have to run now. He knew what happened to men in his line of work when they could no longer function. They ended up like Shawn had.

Silenced forever.

But that wasn't going to happen to him. He'd take care of Kathi and then he'd be on his way. And he knew just how to get to her. Foolproof. Too bad he hadn't thought of it sooner. Then he'd still have his life.

All he had to do was get to the one thing she cared more about than life itself. After all, Kathi was a mother.

"HAS ANYONE SEEN Mom?" Langley asked, as he made a second round of the sprawling house. "She's not upstairs, and she's not in her bedroom or the sewing room."

"She was in the kitchen earlier," Lacy said, "talking about what she wanted to cook for Ryder's dinner. She wanted it to be special."

"Well, I don't see her around now, and Betsy's not here, either."

Langley's wife, Danielle, came through the back door. "Your mother wasn't in the garden, and her car is gone. You don't suppose she took Betsy and went into town, do you?"

"I don't know who she would have gone with. I just left Dillon, and Branson's already in town."

"She might have forgotten and gone by herself," Lacy said. "She's so independent."

Dillon paced the kitchen. "I reminded her just this morning that she was not to leave the ranch by herself."

Lacy walked to the back door and looked out. "She was so upset about the warrant for Ryder's arrest that she may have forgotten your warning."

"I'm calling Branson," Langley said. "And then I'm calling Higgins at the supermarket. If she went anywhere, it was probably to pick up more groceries."

"You don't really think she's in danger, do you?" Danielle walked over to stand by her husband. "I mean, surely no one would hurt a woman and her grandchild. Everyone in Kelman knows her."

"I think she's fine," Langley said, already punching in Branson's phone number. "I'm just following Branson's orders, the way Mom should have."

"I just wish she'd said something," Lacy said. "It's not like her to go off without saying a word to anyone."

"But she's never had a son arrested before." Danielle brushed her thick, dark bangs away from her face. "She's out of her mind with worry. She might have just grabbed up Betsy and left without thinking about it, the way she's always been able to do."

"And the way she'll be able to do again," Langley said, "just not yet."

MARY RANDOLPH pushed the grocery basket carrying her granddaughter down the crowded aisle of Higgins Supermarket. *Bananas, vanilla wafers, extra milk. Bananas, vanilla wafers, extra milk.* She recited a silent mantra of the list as she walked down the crowded aisles.

Her first stop was in the produce section. Bananas. She picked up a bunch and dropped them into her basket. She had to make Ryder banana pudding. He loved it.

Ryder. Her baby, and he was going to jail. It couldn't be happening, and yet it was.

"Na-na-na-na-na." Betsy tried to turn around in the wire seat and grab the yellow fruit.

Mary took Betsy's hands in hers. "Sit still, sweetie. Grandma can't play today. We just have to hurry back home and make a banana pudding for your daddy's dinner. Your daddy loves banana pudding." Her voice cracked. Betsy stared at her as if she could tell something was dreadfully wrong.

"Vanilla wafers and milk." She repeated the words, first in her head and then out loud. *Keep focused. Don't fall apart. Just get what I need and drive back to the Burning Pear. Home to fix Ryder's last dinner as a free man.*

She moved through the store, head down. She didn't want to talk to anyone. They might already know. If they didn't, they'd know soon enough. Some of them might even believe Ryder was guilty. Only how could they? He was a good boy. He'd always been a good boy.

"Da-da-da ga-boo."

"Yes, baby. Don't you worry about a thing. Your grandma is going to be with you. No matter what happens, I'll be right here."

She paid for the groceries and then walked outside. She balanced Betsy in her left arm and held the plastic grocery bag in her right hand.

"Let me help you with that."

"No, I'm fine."

"That's a cute baby you have there."

"Thank you." Any other time, she'd have stayed to chat, even though she'd never seen this man before. But today she had to hurry home. "She's my granddaughter."

"I know. Betsy, isn't it?"

"How did you know that?"

"I know a lot about you, Mrs. Randolph."

She felt something jab against her ribs. She turned and saw the object. A gun.

"Get away from me," she ordered.

"Not today."

Chapter Fourteen

Mary Randolph stared at the gun. This wasn't happening. It couldn't be happening. Not in Kelman. Not today, of all days. She lifted her gaze to the man's face. It was hard and evil. She hugged Betsy to her chest.

"Take my purse. I don't have much cash in it, but take what I have." She tore the shoulder bag from her arm and thrust it toward him. "Take my jewelry, too. My watch and my—" Her heart shattered at the thought of this horrid man taking the wedding ring her husband had placed on her finger so many years ago.

But what was a ring, when there was Betsy to think about? "Take my wedding ring. Take whatever you want, just let me and Betsy go. Surely you don't want to hurt a baby."

Betsy tried to wiggle free from her arms. When Mary wouldn't let her, she started to fuss.

"Get in the car, lady, and don't try anything stupid. I'll be right behind you with my gun pointed at the child. If you make one wrong move..." He aimed the gun at Betsy. "One wrong move and *pop*."

Mary looked around for a friendly face. Someone had to be watching. Someone had to help. This wasn't the big city. It was Kelman, Texas, and she knew everyone in town.

"Move it. I don't have all day. By the time I count to five, I want this car moving. One…two."

Mary was shaking now, so badly she could barely manage to get Betsy in the car seat. And still there was no one in sight. Nothing moving except an old gray hound moseying down the sidewalk.

"Three…"

She fastened Betsy in. The man jumped into the back seat while she hurried around the front of the car and scooted behind the wheel. She had to stay calm. Do nothing to alarm the man. Nothing to make him pull the trigger.

"Four…"

Trembling, she fitted the key into the ignition and turned. The engine roared to life. She pulled away from the curb before the man muttered, "Five."

"Why are you doing this?"

"I have my reasons."

"Then just take me. Let me put the baby out of the car in front of one of the shops. Someone will pick her up and take care of her. Please."

"Save your breath, Mary. Betsy is the most important part of this operation."

Oh, no. She was crying now, and she hated to show weakness in front of this beast. But none of that mattered. Nothing mattered except protecting her precious granddaughter.

"Don't hurt Betsy. That's all I ask. Just don't hurt my baby."

"I don't plan to, unless you force me. You or Betsy's mother."

"Then why won't you let me leave her someplace she'll be cared for?"

"Because I need her. She's the bait. Once Kathi Sable finds out I have her baby, she'll come running to me. I don't know why I didn't think of this a long time ago."

"What did Kathi do to you?"

"Ruined my life. Lost my job for me, and everything else that mattered."

"You're the man who killed Shawn Priest, aren't you?"

"You catch on *real* fast, for an old broad. You keep playing smart, and you'll walk out of this alive. You and the little one. I'm not a monster. I'm just a man who happens to be a perfectionist, and the only job I ever blew, I blew because of Kathi Sable and a two-bit policeman with a yellow streak."

"You won't get away with this."

"Wrong. I *will* get away. I'll fly right out of this country and into one where they don't give a damn what I've done as long as I come with cash to pay for my booze and my women. My plans are all in place. Like I told you, I'm a perfectionist."

Mary drove, her eyes wet with tears, fear rolling and crashing inside her, but she forced herself to think. There had to be a way out of this, and she would have to find it. Betsy's future depended on her.

"We'll be going north, but we'll take the back

roads. Just turn when I tell you, and don't make eye contact with anyone else on the road.''

"We need to stop and buy food. The baby will have to eat.''

"You have milk, vanilla wafers and bananas. A baby can live on that.''

Mary checked the rearview mirror. Betsy was squirming in her car seat, trying to reach the toy radio that had fallen out of her reach. The man picked it up and handed it to her. She stared at him and puckered up. Thankfully she didn't cry.

Instead, she took the toy and punched the red button. The sounds of "Old McDonald" filled the car. A few seconds later, Betsy's head drooped. The ride and the familiar music had lulled her right to sleep.

Now it was just Mary and the madman awake as they drove along an almost deserted farm road. Ryder would be getting home soon. She was supposed to be cooking dinner for him. Earlier today, she had thought it would be the worst day of her life. Now she knew for sure it was.

KATHI FELT the sickening grind in her stomach the moment they pulled up at Arlo's. He was standing outside, but he wasn't alone. A uniformed law officer was standing beside him, and a squad car was parked in front of the house.

"I thought they were going to let you turn yourself in," she said.

"I guess they couldn't wait."

"Your brothers must not know. You said they wanted to be with you when you were arrested."

Arlo left the porch and rushed toward them. The

cop was a few steps behind him. Ryder stepped to the ground just as Arlo rounded the front of the truck.

"I don't know how to tell you this, Ryder." His voice sounded an alarm as surely as if the cop had turned on his siren. Kathi clutched Ryder's arm.

"This isn't about my arrest, is it?"

"No." Arlo hesitated. "Your mom and Betsy went into town this afternoon to pick up some groceries. They didn't come back."

Kathi's legs turned to water, her blood to ice. "What do you mean, they didn't come back?"

"I'm sorry, Kathi. I know how tough this is on you and Ryder."

Ryder wrapped an arm about her shoulders, but he needed the comfort as much as she did. Only she had nothing to give. She forced herself to listen as Arlo explained what he knew.

"Mr. Higgins was emptying trash in the bin behind the supermarket when he saw your mom driving off. He said it looked as if there was a man in the back seat with Betsy. He didn't get that good a look at him. He just thought it was one of your brothers."

"Where are my brothers?" Ryder's voice was strained, but he was rock-hard beside her. Even his face looked as if it had been chiseled from granite.

"They're at the Burning Pear, waiting for a call. Officer Gaines is here to escort you over there."

"Over there and then to jail?"

Arlo shook his head. "No, now that Betsy and your mom have been abducted, they've changed their mind about arresting you. They can no longer ignore Kathi's story of what she saw that night."

"Isn't that big of them? And why were Mom and Betsy out alone?"

Arlo clapped Ryder on the back. "Don't waste your energy searching for someone to blame. Just go home and help your brothers find a way to get them returned safely."

Kathi climbed back in the truck. Now she was finally free to go to the Burning Pear. Because her daughter wasn't there.

THE KITCHEN at the Burning Pear served as headquarters. Kathi tried to imagine what it must have been like on ordinary days when Betsy sat in the heirloom high chair eating her dinner and entertaining her dad and all her cowboy uncles. Then there would have been laughter and conversation, the sound of utensils being stirred in a pot. The sound of Betsy banging her hands on the worn tray.

Today it was as if the room had been drained of everything good. The talk was in quiet, drawn voices, and it was void of laughter. The only time everyone jumped to attention was when the phone rang. But it was always one of the neighbors who'd heard of their misfortune and wanted to see if they could do anything to help.

Now Kathi sat at the kitchen table, fondling a soft, toy cow that Ryder said was one of Betsy's favorites. Ryder sat next to her, and his brothers were all around, still trying to put the missing pieces of the puzzle together and talking strategy. Only what good was strategy when no one had called, and the police had still not located Mary Randolph's car?

"Can I get you something, Kathi? One of the

neighbors just sent over a plate of sandwiches and
Ashley warmed a pot of soup.''

She looked up to find Branson's wife, Lacy, standing over her. ''No, I couldn't eat.''

Lacy pulled up a chair and sat down on the other
side of her. All of the Randolphs, Branson included,
had treated her like part of the family from the second she'd stepped through the door. She knew it was
because of Ryder and Betsy, but still, it was nicer
treatment than she deserved.

There was a bond in this room that erased dividing
lines. She was part of the trauma. She was part of
the team. She was part of the Randolph family. At
least for now.

The phone rang. Everyone jumped as if a cannon
had been fired. Ryder grabbed the receiver and answered, though they could all hear both sides of the
conversation through a special speaker system that
Branson had set up. One that didn't let the caller
know he was being broadcast.

''Ryder Randolph.''

''Ryder, this is Joshua Kincaid. I just heard about
your mom and your daughter.''

''Then you'll understand that we're trying to keep
the phone lines open.''

''I grew up with your dad, Ryder, and your mom
and I have known each other for most of our lives.
If I have anything you can use, all you have to do is
ask. Anything. The jet. Manpower. Money. Anything.''

''I'm grateful for the offer. Right now, we're waiting to hear from the abductor. And every cop in the
state is looking for my mom's car.''

"Then just keep me posted, Ryder. I'd appreciate it."

"There is one thing you could do, Kincaid."

"Anything."

"Tell us what Shawn was into that caused someone to kill him."

"If I knew anything, I'd tell you."

"Would you? Because I think you do know something. You and Julia Rodrigue. Is Peyton Ferran involved in this?"

There was a long pause on the other end of the phone line. "Bull Ruffkins and Shawn Priest both did some work for Ferran. There were problems. That's all I know, Ryder."

"That could help."

"Just be careful. Be real careful. And if there's anything I can do, let me know."

Ryder finished the conversation and hung up the phone. They had to keep the lines open.

"SO PEYTON FERRAN is likely in on this?" Branson said.

"Kathi and I thought as much when Julia was so hesitant to talk."

"Hesitant, and yet you could tell she wanted to tell us more," Kathi said.

"Except I'm not sure what connection he had with Bull and Shawn," Dillon said.

"I think maybe you do, Dillon. I think you're the man who called it all along. We just forgot to listen to what you were saying. Bull is a bookie. If Joshua Kincaid was actually allowing illegal betting on his premises, Bull might be the man who was handling the bets and Ferran might be the man running the operation. Shawn must have gotten involved with them.''

Branson leaned back against the counter. ''You just may have something, little brother.''

THE NEXT CALL was from the police. Mary Randolph's car had been located just outside Frio Town. The car seat was missing.

''At least we have somewhere to centralize the search,'' Branson said. ''We know the direction they were traveling in when they left Kelman.''

''We know more than that,'' Langley said. ''The guy took the car seat. That means he plans to keep Betsy safe. At least, that's what it means to me.''

''And to me, too.'' Danielle walked over to stand by her husband. ''I believe Mary and Betsy are both safe. We just have to find a way to get them back.''

Langley took her in his arms and held her close. Her body shook with sobs, and Kathi had to fight to keep her own tears from starting again. A room full of people, and they all loved her daughter as much as they loved Mary Randolph. And she had brought this horror down on them, and on Betsy.

''Everybody's getting all worked up when we need to be calm and rational,'' Branson said. ''This is not a random abduction. But I'm not sure it's someone who just wants to keep Kathi quiet, either. If anything would make her tell what she knows, it would be kidnapping her baby. She'd squeal in a second to save her child.''

''So what do you think is behind it?''

''Right now my guess would be revenge and a

man who's fallen over the edge. This is not the same kind of operation that killed Shawn. It's not clean. Not professional. Kidnappings seldom are. They bring in every law officer for miles around and frequently the FBI.''

The phone rang again. Ryder laid his hand on the receiver.

''You know what to do,'' Branson said.

Ryder picked it up and Branson set the speaker and taping mechanism in motion.

''Ryder Randolph. Can I help you?''

His question was met by excruciating moments of silence. Finally a male voice came through. ''I have Betsy and her grandmother. They're alive and unharmed.''

''How do I know that?''

''You take my word for it. Listen fast. I want Kathi Sable to meet me. I'll tell her where when I call back. I want one million dollars cash, in hundreds, in a plain black suitcase. Do as I say and no one will get hurt. Cross me, and baby and grandma will be history.''

''It will take a while to get—'' The connection was cut off with a resounding thud.

''Were you able to trace the call?'' Langley asked.

''Not quite. I needed a little more time. The man obviously knows what he's doing.''

''Get the money,'' Ryder said to no one in particular.

''You can't play games with this man,'' Dillon protested. ''We have to have a plan of action. We have to have police backup. Otherwise it's suicide. Tell him that, Branson.''

"You just did. But I agree."

"I wish we knew for sure who we're dealing with," Langley said.

Ryder pounded his fist into the wall. "I'm getting the money. When he calls back, the cash will be here, ready to go."

KATHI SAT at the table with her head buried in her hands. It had been four hours since the initial call from the kidnapper. It seemed like years. The big house at Burning Pear had become a tomb.

"Can I fix you a sandwich?" Danielle asked, stopping to place a hand on Kathi's shoulder. "I know you're not hungry, but you should try to eat something."

"Just coffee."

Lacy poured a cup and put it at Kathi's elbow. "Betsy will be all right, Kathi. She just has to be."

"I thought that when I gave her up the first time."

"I know how hard that must have been for you."

"It almost killed me. It would have if I hadn't believed Ryder would make sure she was taken care of."

"And he did. He kept her safe and loved."

"Until I showed up and led the danger back into her life."

The phone rang. Everyone jumped and waited as Ryder picked up the receiver. This time it was the Fort Worth Police Department with the first piece of concrete evidence. There were prints left on the weight bar that had been used to knock the gun from Ryder's hands. The prints belonged to Bull Ruffkins.

"It looks like we have the identity of the abductor," Branson said. "Now we just have to find him."

THE NEWS brought a clamor of discussion. It all stopped when the phone rang again. Ryder answered and the voice of the kidnapper came over the speaker.

"Do you have the money?"

"I have it," Ryder answered. "Are my mom and daughter safe?"

"Yes."

"Then let me talk to my mother."

"You can take my word for it."

"Why would I? If you want this deal to go through, put my mother on the phone."

They all waited, silently. The air in the room felt thick and suffocating. Finally it was Mary's voice that filled her own kitchen back at Burning Pear.

"I'm here, Ryder. I'm not hurt. Neither is Betsy. She's sleeping now, but she's not hurt. Please, just give this man what he wants so I can bring Betsy home."

"Will do, Mom." His voice broke on the words. "Just hang in there. We're coming."

A chime sounded in the background, sweet and rich, like a church bell. One chime and the beginning of another. Then the sound of the receiver being slammed down filled the room.

Kathi glanced at the clock on the kitchen wall. It was exactly seven o'clock. She closed her eyes as tears squeezed out. "I know where they are," she said. "I know where Bull Ruffkins took Mrs. Randolph and Betsy."

Before she could finish telling the Randolphs about the clock in the tractor-repair shop that belonged to Cyrus Ruffkins, Bull called again. This time he gave full instructions for how he wanted the exchange made.

Kathi and a million dollars in exchange for Mary Randolph and Betsy.

KATHI SAT with Ryder in one of Kincaid's cars in the crowded parking lot of a big Fort Worth hotel as the crescent moon slipped behind a layer of clouds. She had a suitcase full of hundred-dollar bills beside her. What the Randolphs couldn't come up with on the spur of the moment, Joshua Kincaid had. He'd also flown them all to Fort Worth in his private jet.

They were giving the abductor exactly what he'd asked for. That and a little bit more.

Bull Ruffkins would drive up in a black Mustang and park near the street. She was to walk to it, open the passenger door and get in the car. If she arrived with the money, he would take the suitcase and let her go. After he was out of the country, he would call and tell them where to find Mary Randolph and Betsy.

But everyone knew he had no intention of releasing Kathi alive. This was a trap. Only it was Bull Ruffkins who was about to be snared.

Ryder pulled her into his arms. "Are you sure you want to go through with this?"

"I'm positive. I want to catch him dead to rights, the money in his hand. I want this over with completely so that I can go on with my life."

He tucked a thumb under her chin and tilted her

face upward until he could look into her eyes. "Do you know how much I love you?"

"Yes. I didn't for a long time, but I do now. And I love you." She glanced at her watch. "Do you think the police have Mary and Betsy out of the repair shop by now?"

"I'm sure they're in the police car riding to safety. They'll be calling Branson any minute, if they haven't already."

"I'd feel a lot better about this if we knew for certain they were safe."

The headlights of a car came into view as it turned the corner near the parking lot. The small black car slowed and pulled in, stopping near the street.

"I guess it's time I got moving." She touched the door handle.

Ryder grabbed her arm. "Don't take any chances, Kathi. Please don't do anything but what you and Branson agreed on. If it doesn't work, drop to the ground, just like we practiced."

"I'm cool, Ryder." She touched her fingers to the pistol that rested in her pocket—just in case. "I'm cool."

She squeezed his hand one last time. And then she got out of the truck and walked toward a black Mustang and a killer.

She was to start toward the car and then drop the suitcase. The latch would fly open and the money would fall out. He'd come after it. Then the police who were already in place, crouched in the trunks of cars scattered about the parking lot, would jump out and surround the car.

They'd have their man. It would all be over.

She approached the Mustang, ready to drop the bag and duck behind the car that had been parked in place earlier. The car with armed police inside. She strained for a view of the driver. The moon sneaked from behind the clouds, spreading a silvery glow over the lot.

There was a face pressed against the side window of the car. A face, but it wasn't a man's. It was the face of a baby.

Chapter Fifteen

Ryder watched from the truck as Kathi tugged the black suitcase across the parking lot. Step after step. She knew what to do. They'd rehearsed it time and again. Stop a few yards out, just in front of a parked car. Drop the case while pulling the nearly invisible cord that would make it fall open. Then, as the money spilled out, she was to duck under the car.

Branson and the cops would do the rest. When the man jumped out to get the money, they'd take him. In the meantime, Langley, Dillon and a team of cops would be at the shop rescuing his mom and Betsy.

A perfect plan, if it worked.

Only Kathi should be stopping now. She should be pulling the cord. She was going too close to the car. Something was wrong.

KATHI STARED at the car. The man's face was in the window now, watching her. His face, behind a baby's. Betsy. Her Betsy. Her heart jumped to her throat.

This wasn't part of the plan. Betsy wasn't supposed to be in the car. She was supposed to be back at the repair shop being rescued.

If she pulled the cord, the money would fall out. Bull would jump from the car, but there would be gunfire. Betsy could get killed.

She stopped walking. She couldn't go through with this. She'd have to get in the car so that he'd give them Betsy. But what if he didn't? She stood, too terrified to move.

The man took the baby from the window. He revved the engine and inched forward. He was about to drive away with her baby. "Don't go," she screamed. She ran toward the car, tugging the suitcase. But it was so heavy. The car inched forward. "Don't go."

He stopped. Her breath burned in her lungs, but she ran the last few feet and yanked open the passenger side door. Betsy was there, in her car seat. Safe. Kathi struggled for air. "Give me my baby, and I'll give you the money."

"Get in the car, Kathi."

"No. Not until you put Betsy outside the car. I'll go with you. Betsy isn't going."

"I said get in the car, or I'll kill you right here."

"The way Kent Quay was supposed to do, after I saw the two of you shoot down Shawn Priest in the parking lot of his apartment building?"

"Exactly. Only the 'two of us' didn't shoot Kent Quay. I did. Kent never earned his keep." His face twisted into a terrifying scowl. "Get in the car, Kathi. *Now.*"

She pulled the cord. The case flew open. She took a stack of hundred-dollar bills and waved them in the air. "If you want this money, you'll hand me Betsy. Ryder is here and so is his brother the sheriff. They both have guns. If you shoot me and get out to pick up the money, they'll kill you before you get away. They don't know you have the baby with you. That wasn't the deal you offered."

She watched his expression change. She had him. "Me and the money, Bull, just like you wanted. All you have to do is hand me Betsy still strapped into her seat. I'll sit her down on the ground and Ryder will pick her up the second we drive away. And they won't fire on you if I'm in the car."

"Take her." He handed her Betsy, car seat and all.

"Bye-bye-bye, na-na." Betsy talked and laughed and put her fingers in Kathi's hair as she took her in her arms. Her world was about to come to an end, but all she could do was stare at her beautiful baby girl.

"Mommy loves you. Remember that." Her voice quavered. She kissed Betsy's sweet cheek. "Remember always that Mommy loves you." She didn't try to stop the flow of tears as she set Betsy behind a parked car, out of harm's way.

"Get in the car now." A string of ugly curses followed Bull's command.

Get in the car and give up the baby she'd waited so long to find. Get in the car with the madman who'd stalked her for a year to keep her from telling something she didn't even know. Get in the car and never see Ryder or her baby again.

She reached into her pocket and touched the cold, hard handle of the pistol.

"I don't think so, Bull. I just don't think so."

She raised the gun. He jumped out of the car and she saw the weapon in his hand as he ducked below the fender. The sound of the bullet was deafening. Only she hadn't pulled the trigger.

"NICE WORK, Ryder. Shooting those tin cans wasn't such a waste of time after all."

Branson stepped from out of the darkness. Bull stood and then fell against the hood of the car as crimson blood from a gun wound in his shoulder spilled over the black paint.

Betsy wailed at the top of her lungs. Still dizzy from the fast turn of events, Kathi dropped to her knees and unbuckled the kicking baby. She cried all the louder.

"I think she wants her dad," Ryder said, taking her from Kathi's arms. She hushed immediately. He put his arm around Kathi and led her away as the night filled with the scream of police sirens and the flash of blue lights.

Safe in her daddy's arms, Betsy turned to smile at Kathi.

"Betsy Randolph, meet your mom," Ryder said. "She's home to stay."

KATHI SAT in the big rocker in the Randolph nursery, holding her precious baby in her arms. Betsy was asleep, nestled against Kathi's breast, but Kathi couldn't bear to put her down. Her arms had ached for this privilege, and it was all she dreamed it would be.

Ryder stepped through the door. He stood looking

at her in the dim light, and she could feel his love surrounding her and their daughter.

"Is it over?" she asked.

"All over. Bull spilled his guts. We had most of it figured right. Bull and Kent Quay were the two men you saw at the murder scene. They both worked for Peyton Ferran. He was running a money-laundering and gambling operation using Joshua Kincaid's clubs as a front. Shawn wanted out. Peyton decided he knew too much. So the hit was ordered."

"But why didn't Kent kill me the day he found me?"

"Because he was convinced you didn't recognize him when he showed up to finish you off. He believed your story. Peyton told them to let you go as long as you ran like they said and didn't go to the police or to me. But Bull panicked when he saw the two of us together. He tried to run you down and instead got me. Peyton was furious with him."

"And why was Shawn's body buried at the Burning Pear?"

"Peyton was afraid Shawn had told me something about the operations, but he didn't want to kill me. The brother of a well-known Texas senator was too high-profile. So he did the next best thing. He buried the body on my land. If I talked, he was going to leak the location of the body to the cops. Then my story would lose all credibility. It would look as if I were just trying to cover up a murder I had committed."

"A very tangled web Peyton Ferran wove."

"Too tangled. That's what tripped him up. When Shawn's body was finally found and you came back to testify about what you'd seen the day Shawn Priest was shot, he ordered Bull to kill you. Only Kent found out. By then he'd had enough killing. He came to warn you, followed you and Bull to the campground, but Bull killed him instead. Peyton went berserk and told Bull he was through with him.''

"And that's when this became personal," Kathi said.

"That's it. Personal and even more deadly. Bull wasn't stupid. He'd done the hit on Shawn, so he knew what it meant when Peyton Ferran was through with you. And in his mind, this was all your fault. Yours and Kent Quay's.''

Betsy stirred in her arms. She hugged her tightly.

"Are you ready to put her down and go to bed?"

"I'm not sure I'll ever be ready to put her down. But I guess I should get some sleep.''

"I think so. After all, you'll have the rest of your life to spend with your daughter." He knelt beside them. "To spend with your daughter and her daddy. That is, if you'll have me.''

"Is this a proposal?"

"Do you want to wait for a more romantic time? Do you want a ring and champagne and some exotic location? If you do, just say the word.''

"No. I can't think of any more romantic spot in the world than the nursery where our baby girl is sleeping peacefully." She trailed a finger down his cheek. "I love you, Ryder Randolph. I have since the day I met you. And the answer is yes.''

Epilogue

"Happy Birthday to you, happy birthday to you, happy birthday, dear Betsy, happy birthday to you."

Betsy clapped her hands as the big white candle flickered in the center of a chocolate cake with fluffy white frosting. Kathi stood by Ryder, surrounded by her new family. It was Betsy's first birthday. And she was here.

Pure joy danced through her veins.

"Can I help her blow out the candle?" Petey asked, sidling up next to the birthday girl.

"I should say so," Kathi said. "What kind of birthday celebration would it be if Betsy's big, strong cousin wasn't here to help?"

He laughed and puckered up. When he blew, Betsy, as always, imitated him. Together they managed to extinguish the flame.

"I think this is the very best celebration we've ever had," Mary Randolph said.

Langley wrapped an arm about his mother's shoulders. "Has anyone heard that before?"

They all laughed.

"Well, at least we don't have to look at any big

gaudy bouquets from Joshua Kincaid's," Dillon said. "The man is finally behind bars where he belongs."

"He did help us, though, in the end," Kathi reminded him.

"Too little, too late. And now he's locked away with his crony Peyton Ferran. And Bull Ruffkins is the one who's sealing the jailhouse door behind them. Squealing his head off, and he's still going to prison. The state of Texas will be a better place."

"The state of Texas will be a better place for another reason." Ryder put his hands on Kathi's shoulders. "I'm giving up rodeo competition for good. It's time I grew up and took a real job."

"Don't tell me you're going to stay home and help me run the ranch?" Langley said.

Ryder winced. "I'm not growing up that much. I'm thinking of opening a rodeo school, kind of a boot camp for those thinking of hitting the circuit, or those who've been injured and need to work back up to their peak level. And in the summer, I'll bring out some city kids for a few weeks and teach them to ride and rope."

Dillon tilted his head and studied Ryder. "You're serious, aren't you?"

"As serious as a dog digging up a bone. And the rodeo life is not all I'm thinking of giving up."

Branson hooked his thumbs into his belt loops. "Don't tell me you're thinking of giving up chasing women?"

Kathi turned and wrapped an arm about Ryder's waist. "Let's just say that if he comes home with a stray hair on his shoulder, he'd better have a horse to match."

"You heard her," Ryder said. "But why would I look anywhere else when I've already found the best? You are all invited to the wedding."

Everyone hugged each other at once. Toasts and laughter and kissing. The way a family should be. When it was Branson's turn, he hugged Kathi extra tight. "I was wrong about you. You're the best thing that ever happened to my little brother. Oops! I've got to quit referring to him that way. He grew up into quite a man. I suspect you can take credit for a lot of that." He kissed Kathi on the cheek. "Welcome to the family."

"Coming from you, that means a lot."

But when Kathi moved out of the circle of well-wishers, she caught sight of Mary Randolph standing all alone. Her eyes were wet with tears.

Kathi walked over and stopped beside the wonderful woman who was Betsy's grandmother and soon to be her mother-in-law. "Is something wrong?"

"No." She wrapped an arm around Kathi's waist and embraced her. "My family is all here. All safe. All my boys finally settled and happy. All in love with good women who love them, too." She wiped the tears away with her sleeve. "Everything is right."

Kathi looked back at Betsy, smiling and sticking her fingers into the cake icing. Ryder was beside her, handsome and strong. The perfect cowboy daddy.

And tears moistened Kathi's eyes, as well. She couldn't agree with Mary more. She had her baby, and she had Ryder. She was home to stay.

Everything was right.

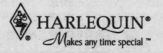

Daddy's little girl... **THAT'S MY BABY!** by

Vicki Lewis Thompson

Nat Grady is finally home—older and wiser. When the woman he'd loved had hinted at commitment, Nat had run far and fast. But now he knows he can't live without her. But Jessica's nowhere to be found.

Jessica Franklin is living a nightmare. She'd thought things were rough when the man she loved ran out on her, leaving her to give birth to their child alone. But when she realizes she has a stalker on her trail, she has to run—and the only man who can help her is Nat Grady.

THAT'S MY BABY!

On sale September 2000 at your favorite retail outlet.

HARLEQUIN®
Makes any time special ™

***Don't miss
an exciting opportunity
to save on the purchase of
Harlequin and Silhouette books!***

Buy any two Harlequin or
Silhouette books and save
$10.00 off future Harlequin
and Silhouette purchases

OR

buy any three
Harlequin or Silhouette books
and save **$20.00 off** future
Harlequin and Silhouette purchases.

***Watch for details
coming in October 2000!***

PHQ400

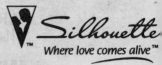

THE SECRET IS OUT!

HARLEQUIN®

INTRIGUE®

presents

TEXAS CONFIDENTIAL

By day these agents are cowboys;
by night they are specialized
government operatives.
Men bound by love, loyalty and the law—
they've vowed to keep their missions
and identities confidential....

Harlequin Intrigue

Harlequin American Romance
(a special tie-in story)

HARLEQUIN®
Makes any time special ™

Visit us at www.eHarlequin.com

HITC

COMING NEXT MONTH

#581 THE BODYGUARD'S ASSIGNMENT by Amanda Stevens
Texas Confidential

Agent Brady Morgan's specialty was witness protection, and Grace Drummond was his downfall. The crime she had witnessed incriminated a dangerous criminal, placing her in serious danger. And the secret Grace kept was one that Brady needed to uncover if he intended to keep them safe and rebuild the love they'd once shared.

#582 AMANDA'S CHILD by Ruth Glick writing as Rebecca York
43 Light Street

When a sperm bank pregnancy endangered virgin Amanda Barnwell's life, Matt Forester appointed himself as her guardian. Caught between two powerful families, Amanda needed Matt's name to protect her unborn child and provide her safety. Only by exposing the true source of the threats could they begin a new life—together.

#583 SAFE BY HIS SIDE by Debra Webb
Secret Identity

"Kate Roberts" didn't remember who she was or how she'd found special-agent-in-hiding Jack Raine—but now, a killer was after them both. And though her returning memories hinted she might have been used to betray Jack, she knew there was nowhere she'd be safer than by his side....

#584 UNDERCOVER PROTECTOR by Cassie Miles

Officer Annie Callahan returned home to simplify her life and instead found herself faced with Michael Slade—a man she'd once loved deeply. Now working undercover, Michael knew Annie was in danger from a stalker and possibly more. Revealing his identity was not an option, so he became her fiancé. Could Michael keep Annie safe—and perhaps get her to fall in love with him all over again?

Visit us at www.eHarlequin.com

CNM0800